BRACKENBEAST

BRACKENBEAST

The Secrets of Eden Eld
BOOK 2

Kate Alice Marshall

VIKING

VIKING
An imprint of Penguin Random House LLC, New York

First published in the United States of America by Viking,
an imprint of Penguin Random House LLC, 2021

Visit us online at penguinrandomhouse.com.

Library of Congress Cataloging-in-Publication Data is available.

Printed in the United States of America

ISBN 9780593117057

10 9 8 7 6 5 4 3 2 1

SKY
Design by Kate Renner
Text set in Perrywood MT Std

For Mathew, who was lost awhile in the Wickerwood but found their way home again.

BRACKENBEAST

The Tale of Thirteens

Once upon a time, in the town of Eden Eld, lived three children born on the very same day: Halloween. This was not a coincidence. It was fate. For Eden Eld hid a terrible secret.

Long ago, its founders struck a bargain with the mysterious People Who Look Away, three strange beings led by the loathsome Mr. January. Eden Eld would enjoy prosperity, peace, and safety, but in return Mr. January and his two sisters demanded a terrible price: three thirteen-year-olds would be taken every thirteen years on Halloween night and transformed into a magical key. When the thirteenth key was collected, the People Who Look Away could open the door into their realm of gray.

Twelve times the people of Eden Eld offered up their children as sacrifices. But when it came time to craft the thirteenth key, something changed. For Eleanor and Pip and Otto were lucky and they were brave, and most of all they were clever.

With only days before Halloween arrived and the curse came to claim them, the children raced to uncover Eden Eld's secrets. Arrayed against them were Mr. January's three animal servants: the cat-of-ashes, the graveyard dog, and the dreadful rattlebird. Worse still was the January Society, a group of Eden Eld citizens who served Mr. January. Among them was Pip's own mother, who was willing and eager to give her daughter over to the curse.

They were not without resources. For in an old grandfather clock with hands that ran backward, they found a book of fairy tales: Thirteen Tales of the Gray. *Within its pages were stories that contained the clues they needed to stop Mr. January's plan. They might have escaped the curse entirely, but they realized that Mr. January would simply wait, and turn a new generation of children into his final key.*

And so the children struck a bargain with the People Who Look Away. Mr. January and his sisters would each have one more chance to claim Eleanor, Pip, and Otto. If they succeeded, the children would become the missing key. But if they failed, the children of Eden Eld would forever be safe from the People Who Look Away and the dreadful curse.

It has been months since those terrifying days. The children know that soon the first of Mr. January's sisters will come for them. And they will be ready . . .

One

It was raining again. It had rained every day for the last three weeks, and Eleanor was starting to wonder if she should invest in an ark. She clumped along the muddy trail. At least she had a good pair of rubber boots, and it wasn't far to Pip's house from school.

She'd had to stay late so she could go to her Yearbook Club meeting. She had to go to her Yearbook Club meeting because normal kids did extracurricular activities, and those extracurricular activities didn't include "searching for Wrong Things" or "researching ways to break curses" or even "cataloging the magical artifacts hidden in a secret room behind the fireplace in your family's spooky old mansion."

When she'd come to Eden Eld, Eleanor had wanted more than anything for people to think she was normal. She didn't want to be known as the girl who saw things that weren't there, or the girl whose mother had burned their house down, or the girl who lived in the creepy old mansion at the edge of town. She just wanted to be Normal Eleanor.

But then she'd met Pip and Otto, and found out that the strange things she saw were real after all. Pip and Otto called them the Wrong Things, and they were all over Eden Eld. The next few days had been a blur of terror and excitement as they discovered that the three of them were at the center of a curse that had been stealing kids for over a century. By the end of it, Eleanor didn't care about being normal quite so much. But she *did* care about Aunt Jenny and Uncle Ben being worried about her. So she went to Yearbook Club and she did her homework and she told them everything was great.

And she *definitely* didn't mention that there was a trio of magical siblings called the People Who Look Away, led by the wicked Mr. January, trying to kidnap her and her friends to use in their evil ritual.

Eleanor and her friends met up after school whenever they could to research more about the Wrong Things and the People Who Look Away, in the hopes of finding something that could save them. Pip and Otto had offered to wait for her to finish with Yearbook Club, but she'd told them to go on ahead without her. She'd meet them at Pip's house.

Which was why she was alone in the rapidly darkening woods when the rain started to glow.

It started as a faint glimmer that Eleanor almost dismissed as a trick of the light, but as the rain got steadier, so did the glow.

A droplet splashed against the back of her hand and ran shimmering down to the cuff of her jacket.

Her skin prickled. Eden Eld was full of strange things. Most of them wouldn't hurt you, if you stayed away. But some of them were hungry, or angry, or just dangerous the way a cliff is dangerous—it doesn't want you to fall, but that doesn't make landing hurt less.

She picked up her pace. It wasn't far to Pip's house. She could handle a little glowing rain.

Off among the trees, something hooted, a low warning sound. *Just an owl*, she told herself. *It was just an owl.*

The rattling moan that followed definitely wasn't.

Eleanor started running. Her backpack, stuffed with textbooks, slowed her down and bounced painfully against the small of her back.

The weird light made the air seem to shiver and ripple. She could barely see anything but the streaking colors of the rain—but there was *something* off among the trees. It was moving with her, keeping perfect pace without making a sound. The glimmering rain dazzled her, making it impossible to see anything but the creature's shadowy form.

She ran faster. So did the shadow. Her breath was sharp and cold in her throat. Her boots slapped against the muddy ground—and then her foot jetted out from under her, hitting a slick of thick mud.

Eleanor hit the ground backpack-first and flailed. She flipped herself back over in time to hear bushes shake and snap as whatever was hunting her charged forward.

A scream tore from her throat. She ditched her heavy backpack and sprinted away, plunging into the trees. Branches clawed at her face and arms.

Her foot caught against a root. She made a wild grab for the nearest tree trunk and managed to stay upright. She panted, looking desperately around her. The woods were empty. No creature. No shadow-thing. Just the steady plinking of the rain.

"Eleanor!" Pip's voice came from close by.

"Pip! I'm here!" she shouted back. "There's something in the woods!"

Moments later, Pip came tromping toward Eleanor, her walking stick—made of solid ash and excellent for fighting magical beasts—held in a tight grip. The rain had set her red hair into a frantic frizz around her pale, freckled face, but her expression was fierce. Otto, whose tight, dark curls were shimmering with the rain, thrashed his way through the underbrush.

"What's wrong? What's after you?" Pip asked, drawing in close and squinting at the woods. Everything shifted and blurred behind the weird light of the rain.

"I don't know. I saw a shadow. It was big," Eleanor said. "I think."

"Look!" Otto cried out. He pointed as something darted past them, low to the ground. "Is that it?"

"It was bigger than that," Eleanor said, but she couldn't help the uncertainty in her voice. What *had* she seen?

"Whatever this one is, it's glowing," Pip said grimly, pointing the end of her stick in the direction the small shadow had gone. The light seemed brighter up ahead, past a huge pine tree.

Eleanor crept forward behind Pip, who held her walking stick—or hittin' stick, as she liked to call it—at the ready. The light at the base of the tree pulsed like a heartbeat.

"Yahhh!" Pip cried, and leaped around the side of the tree. And stood there, brow creased.

"What is it?" Eleanor asked. She stepped around the tree.

A salamander the length of her foot blinked up at her. Its translucent skin glimmered like the rain, blues and pale purples swirling and rippling. Tiny mushrooms grew around it, and they were glowing, too.

"Don't try anything," Pip warned it. The salamander did not seem inclined to defy her. It stared. After a moment, it blinked again.

"Pip! Eleanor! Check this out! There's more of them!" Otto cried, and burst out from behind a bush, holding another of the glowing salamanders in both hands. Its hind legs dangled. It looked less evil than vaguely confused about its present condition.

Pip gave it a narrow-eyed look and menaced the creature with her walking stick. "Watch out, Otto. It's probably poisonous. Or carnivorous. Or"—she paused, considering—"*scheming.*"

"I don't think so," Otto said with a frown, turning the

salamander so he could peer into its face. It stuck out its fat tongue and licked its own eye.

Eleanor sighed and wiped the rain from her glasses with the edge of her sleeve, which only succeeded in smearing it into wet streaks. She must have imagined the thing being giant and frightening because the salamanders definitely weren't either of those things.

Pip lowered the walking stick. "At least put it down until we know what it is," Eleanor pleaded.

"Okay, fine," Otto said with an annoyed huff and set the salamander down. It stayed where he put it but bounced up and down a few times. Otto dropped into a crouch to watch, his tight curls flopping over his face. "So cool," he said.

"Wrong Things aren't cool," Pip said, but Otto just made a shooing motion.

Otto and Pip were best friends. They'd known each other for all of their thirteen years. Eleanor was the newcomer to the group, but she tried not to let that bother her. After all, they shared a unique bond: they'd all been born on Halloween, and they were all descended from the founders of Eden Eld. And that made them cursed.

Last Halloween, the curse had almost taken them. They'd avoided it temporarily, but they knew that they weren't safe for good. Eleanor and her friends had to be on their guard.

"I like them," Otto said. In Pip's opinion, stated loudly and often, he was not sufficiently on his guard at all. "I think I'm going to call them glimmanders. Or glimmermanders. What do you think?"

"I think they're going to try to eat your face," Pip told him, but without much conviction.

Eleanor couldn't see how these placid little creatures could possibly be part of Mr. January and his sisters' schemes. Just to be safe, she took out the flat shard of crystal that hung around her neck on a chain. She'd used it before to see the true nature of the Wrong Things and other hidden magical secrets, and now she lifted it to her eye, peering through it. The salamanders didn't look any different.

"I don't think they're a threat, Pip," she said gently.

"I'm not stupid. I know they're not a threat *this second*. But we don't know anything about them!" Pip glared at her—and then looked down at the ground, taking a deep breath. Eleanor knew she was counting to ten in her head. It was supposed to help her control her anger. Judging by how often Eleanor and Otto found themselves getting glowered at, and how many snapped pencils rattled around in Pip's backpack, it wasn't terribly effective.

"It's my fault. I freaked out over nothing," Eleanor said, trying to smooth things over.

"Yeah, you did," Pip snapped. She stalked away, marching back toward the path.

Otto glanced at Eleanor, wounded worry on his face. Otto had big, dark brown eyes, light brown skin, and a wide, expressive mouth that was quick to smile or frown. That was one of her favorite things about Otto—he never hid what he felt. "Did I say something wrong?" he asked.

"I don't think so," Eleanor replied. "I'm pretty sure she's mad at me. Again." She wasn't like Otto. She thought about every expression, every word, always aware of how she seemed to other people. And right now, she was trying to sound reassuring and confident, even though her stomach was one big knot of anxiety. "It's just hard, you know?"

"No, I don't. And that's the problem, isn't it? I have a totally normal family with awesome parents, so I don't understand what it's like. Right?"

The rain drummed against their shoulders and slicked Eleanor's hair down. She could only shrug helplessly. Pip's mother had been one of the people who tried to give them to Mr. January. That wasn't something you got over in five months. Before that, Eleanor's mother had disappeared—and for months, Eleanor had believed she burned their house down, trapping Eleanor inside and almost killing her. It turned out not to be true, but she was probably the person who most understood what Pip was going through.

She hated this. She hated that Pip was hurting and she hated that it hurt Otto, too. And that she couldn't fix any of it.

Pip, shoulders sagging, trudged back toward them. "Hey, guys. I'm sorry I got mad."

"That's okay," Eleanor said quickly. "We're all on edge.

We don't know when Mr. January's sisters are going to come after us."

"Can I take another look at the salamanders? With your crystal?" Pip asked. She reached out a hand.

"Of course." Eleanor lifted the chain over her head and started to hand it over.

"Stop!" Pip yelled—but Pip hadn't said anything. Not *that* Pip, at least.

Another Pip, identical to the one standing in front of Eleanor, charged through the trees. Eleanor froze. And then she looked down.

The Pip with her hand outstretched was standing on a muddy patch of ground that showed her footprints clearly. Footprints that were pointed the wrong way around.

Two

Eleanor snatched her crystal back, clutching it against her chest. The not-Pip smiled and chuckled softly. "Worth a try," she said, but it wasn't Pip's voice at all.

Not-Pip stepped back, and with that single step she stretched and changed, growing taller and broader, her features sliding and shifting. Otto squeaked and grabbed Eleanor's wrist as Mr. January straightened up with a sigh, no longer gripping Pip's walking stick but the slender silver-capped cane he always carried.

He was a thin, plain-looking man, eerie in his ordinariness. He rolled his shoulders, as if he'd been in a cramped space and was just stepping out, and his shadow bubbled behind him, splitting into three dark forms. The rattlebird, a wicked crow with bones in its feathers that clacked as it flew, flapped into the trees overhead. The graveyard dog sat at its master's side, red eyes glowing as smoke trickled between its yellowed teeth.

And the cat-of-ashes picked her way over to a stump and settled her haunches onto it, yawning widely, a bored expression in her amber eyes.

Eleanor's heart beat wildly. Mr. January wasn't supposed to come after them until next Halloween. What was he doing here?

"Greetings, children," Mr. January said in his honey-sweet voice.

"What do you want?" Eleanor demanded. She gripped Otto's hand tightly. Pip stood on the other side of Mr. January and the beasts, her lips peeled back in a snarl.

"Simply to drop in and see how you little dears are holding up," Mr. January replied, eyes wide with feigned innocence. "You must be ever so anxious. I do hope you've finished your preparations, with things starting so soon."

"What do you mean?" Otto asked suspiciously. "What things?"

Mr. January smiled indulgently. "Why, everything has its season, Otto, and my younger sister's season is upon us. She should be arriving anytime now. She may even be here already. Isn't it exciting? She's going to have such fun with you." He reached out a long finger, as if to caress Eleanor's cheek.

Pip yelled and lunged, swinging the walking stick like a baseball bat right at Mr. January's back. The graveyard dog whirled, but Mr. January was faster—it was like he never moved at all, but he was suddenly facing the other way. He caught the walking stick against his palm, fingers wrapping around it. Pip yanked back hard. His grip stayed steady.

"Now, now. That won't do," he said in a soft and dangerous tone. The rattlebird shook its wings with a horrid *clackclackclack* of bones. The cat-of-ashes crouched, ears flat against her head. The graveyard dog growled, a low rumble that vibrated in Eleanor's chest.

"Don't hurt her!" Eleanor cried.

Pip glared up at Mr. January, but she was shaking.

"I won't hurt her. *That* would be against the rules, and I never break the rules. Especially my own," Mr. January said. His smile widened. And then he clenched his hand over the walking stick.

It shattered.

Splinters of wood flew in all directions. Pip yelped and stumbled back, holding tight to the stubby length of wood that remained. She gaped at its splintered end in horror.

The graveyard dog gave a pleased huff. The rattlebird cackled a laugh. "No more nasty stick for you," it gurgled at her.

The cat-of-ashes hissed in displeasure. "Rough luck, kitten," she muttered. She stretched her toes, raking her claws across the rotten wood of the stump and leaving scorch marks. She might technically work for Mr. January, but she'd helped them before.

Eleanor edged around, dragging Otto with her, and seized

hold of Pip. She pulled her back until she was standing with them, away from Mr. January and his giant hound. "Leave us alone," Eleanor said. Pip was still staring down at her shattered walking stick, eyes wide.

"Very well. I only thought you'd appreciate a bit of warning."

"If you're so helpful, tell us what your sister is planning to do," Eleanor said.

"Now that would be spoiling the fun." Mr. January tsked, brushing little splinters from his fingers with an expression of distaste. "I would suggest you three improve upon your manners. But I don't suppose you have the time. Tick tock."

He twirled his cane. The rattlebird stooped and dived, vanishing once again into his shadow. The graveyard dog leaped, disappearing with a puff of smoke. Mr. January stood waiting for a second, then two, and then cut a glare at the cat-of-ashes, who twitched her tail, sighed, and walked unhurriedly over.

"See you around, kids," she said as she twined once around Mr. January's ankle, and was gone.

"Cats," Mr. January muttered, and then gave a bow. "Give my regards to my sister. If you manage to see her coming," he told them, and then he snapped his fingers—and vanished.

Eleanor sagged. Pip let out a last yell and chucked the ruined walking stick at the space where Mr. January had been a moment before. Otto put an arm around her shoulders. "I'm sorry, Pip," he said mournfully.

"It's just a stupid stick," Pip said, but she wiped her nose with the back of her hand and sniffed. "Jerk."

"That was weird," Eleanor said. She stared down at the foot-prints he'd left—the small, Pip-size ones and the bigger set. "What is he up to?"

"He's trying to scare us," Pip said.

"It's working," Otto replied, flicking his hair back from his face nervously.

"I don't think he wanted to scare us," Eleanor said slowly. "It was like he was really warning us. Letting us know that we need to be on our guard."

"Why would he do that?" Pip asked, skeptical.

"I don't know," Eleanor admitted. It didn't make much sense now that she said it out loud. "But whatever he's up to, I don't think he's lying. Which means that one of his sisters is coming for us. Soon."

"Great. Well, at least the rain stopped glowing," Pip grumbled. "Let's get back to the house. We can figure it out when we're dry."

"Good idea," Eleanor agreed. They made their way back to the path, following the trampled undergrowth from Eleanor's earlier flight. They emerged right where she'd dropped her backpack. She winced as she picked it up. Her homework was going to be a sodden mess. She just hoped her textbooks weren't ruined. Otto helped her brush most of the mud off, and she slung it over one shoulder.

"Hey, um." Pip scuffed her foot against the ground. They turned to her. "I'm sorry I'm in such a bad mood."

"Is it a mood if it lasts more than a month?" Otto asked, teasing.

The corner of Pip's mouth twitched. "I think I get another six weeks before it's officially a personality," she said.

Otto reached out and squeezed her hand once, quickly. Eleanor couldn't help but notice how fleeting their physical contact had gotten even since Halloween, age suddenly making normal things seem strange.

"If Mr. January's sister is here, we need to do more research when we get to your place, Pip," Eleanor said. "Unless you have to get home, Otto."

"Nuh-uh. If I go home I'm going to get dragged into debating whether the dining room should be eggshell or off-white." Otto's family had moved into a bigger house when his mom got pregnant, meaning to remodel it. When they found out they were having triplets, the plans had gotten delayed. But after spending the winter gutting the house one room at a time, it was almost done. All that was left was the painting, which was taking almost as long as the rest of the remodel.

Eleanor nodded. "Pip, do you still have *Thirteen Tales* or did you give it to Otto?" *Thirteen Tales of the Gray* was the book of fairy tales they'd found last Halloween that had helped them escape the curse. It was full of stories that had little hints about the People Who Look Away and the Wrong Things. Eleanor was certain that it had more secrets to reveal, if only they knew how to put the pieces together.

"I've got it," Pip said, sounding evasive.

"Did you finish reading it?" Eleanor asked.

Pip shrugged. "Kind of. Not really. But we're not going to find anything in that book that we haven't already. You've got it memorized at this point."

"It's the only help we've got," Eleanor said. "We should all be reading it. And memorizing it. Otto took it home over Christmas break. You're the only one who hasn't read the whole thing."

"I know what's in it," Pip said defensively. "We went over the stories a million times at Halloween."

"You know who we need? Jack, from the stories," Otto said. "If we could find *him*, we'd be set." Jack was the hero of a lot of the *Thirteen Tales*, along with the hedgewitch and the girl with backward hands.

"I don't think he's a real person," Eleanor replied. "He's . . ." Eleanor waved her hand vaguely, fumbling for the right word.

"More like an amalgamation?" Pip asked. Eleanor blinked at her. "I'm smart. I know words," Pip said, clearly irritated.

Eleanor shook her head. Of course Pip was smart. She was the only one who ever thought otherwise. "No, I was just thinking that's exactly the word I was looking for," Eleanor said. "He acts really inconsistent. In some of the stories he's really nice, and then in others he's more sarcastic and stuff."

With the thick cloud cover and relentless rain, the path beneath the trees was dark as twilight. This time when they fell into silence there was an uneasy edge. The shadows seemed much too close and much too deep, and Eleanor found herself straining to hear the *clackclackclack* of the dreadful rattlebird or the heavy panting of the graveyard dog. But there was only the drumming of the rain and the squishing of their feet in the mud.

And then a frantic scurry of feet and a high-pitched bark.

"Oh boy," Otto said.

"Not again," Pip groaned.

"Get ready," Eleanor said, and they braced themselves.

A small, sodden dog burst out of the brush and barreled toward them.

Three

The dog, a Jack Russell terrier, was dragging a leash that might have once been blue but was now packed with mud. He saw them, barked once, and sat on his haunches.

"Having fun?" Eleanor asked him. His tail thumped the ground wetly. She approached slowly.

"He's gonna bolt," Otto warned. The dog tensed, ears perking toward her.

"Caspian!" came a call from up the trail, followed by splashing footsteps.

Caspian—properly, Prince Caspian—barked again and launched himself toward the bushes at the other end of the trail. Eleanor lunged, but she was too late. Pip sprinted forward and planted her foot on his leash, pulling him up short. "Not so fast, you rascal."

"We got him, Mr. Maughan," Otto called.

Mr. Maughan, a tall man who was the sort of person sweater

vests were invented for, came puffing up a moment later. Caspian yapped and bounced, struggling to free himself.

"Philippa. Eleanor. Otto. What a fortunate happenstance," Mr. Maughan said. His hair was plastered to his scalp, and his jacket was unzipped, leaving the rain to soak into his argyle vest. He held a soggy purple gift bag in one hand, so drenched it was beginning to come apart. He bent to pick up the rogue terrier's leash. "He spotted a squirrel, I believe. Or maybe a rabbit. I didn't get a good look at it. But off he went like a shot."

Caspian, having determined that he was not, in fact, going to escape, trotted to Mr. Maughan's feet and plopped down, panting happily.

"That keeps happening. You should tie that leash to your wrist or something," Otto said.

"He's not used to the woods, that's all. He'll settle down," Mr. Maughan said.

Eleanor doubted that. Mr. Maughan had lived in the small house half a mile from Pip's for the last six weeks, and Caspian had gotten loose four times already.

Eleanor liked Mr. Maughan, though she wasn't sure if that was just because he was on her list of People Definitely Not Involved in the January Society (Revised). He had moved here from Wisconsin and had absolutely no connections with the town whatsoever, as far as they could tell.

"Why are you even out in this weather?" Otto asked, scrunching up his nose.

"I love the sound of the rain in the trees," Mr. Maughan said.

"Besides, if the Prince doesn't get his walk, he eats the walls. Literally. I've spent a fortune on drywall. By the way, Philippa, I met your aunt. Quite the character, isn't she?"

"My aunt?" Pip asked, startled. "You mean Josephine?"

Pip and Otto exchanged stricken glances, and even Eleanor felt a little zip of alarm. She'd never met Aunt Josephine, but she'd heard plenty of stories.

"That's the one," Mr. Maughan said with a chuckle. "You seem surprised."

"I just didn't know she was in town," Pip said carefully. Then she shook her head. "It's fine. She never warns us, that's all. I'll see you around, Mr. Maughan."

He waved goodbye and set off down the path.

"So . . . this is *the* Josephine?" Eleanor asked.

"The very one," Pip said, frowning.

"That's not a bad thing, is it?" Eleanor asked. She dropped her voice to a hushed tone. "Are you worried she's like your mom?" She didn't say *evil*, but they all knew what she meant. Pip's mom had tried to give them to Mr. January, but she'd ended up sucked into another world instead. Josephine was Pip's aunt on her dad's side, not her mom's, but evil adults weren't exactly hard to come by in Eden Eld, so that didn't prove anything.

But Pip laughed. "Oh, gosh, no. Jojo's great. She's *amazing.*"

"She's the *best,*" Otto agreed. "Only the thing is . . ."

"Auntie Jojo is as wonderful as triple fudge brownie ice cream with extra fudge sauce and full-size marshmallows.

Having two bites is amazing—but the third bite is A Problem," Pip explained. "Still better than evil, though."

Just then, they rounded the corner to Pip's house. Eleanor spotted Aunt Josephine's car immediately. It was hard to miss, given that it was bright yellow and painted with giant blue flowers. Boxes and suitcases and bags were crammed into the back, and even the passenger seat was piled high.

They filed inside the house and shifted their dripping to the foyer. "Dad?" Pip called, stripping off her rain gear and kicking her boots toward the rack, splattering mud on the wall as she did. Pip's father appeared. He was wearing slacks and a button-up shirt, which, even with the shirt being wrinkled, was more dressed than Eleanor had seen him recently. He worked from home and had very comfortable pajamas.

"Pip, your aunt is visiting," he said, sounding a bit strained.

"Yeah," Pip said carefully. "She's got a lot of boxes in her car."

"She might be staying awhile," he said mournfully.

"Ohhhh," Pip replied in understanding. Eleanor looked at her blankly. Pip dropped her voice. "Every year or so something goes wrong and Aunt Josephine comes to visit for a *while*. Usually it's because she lost a job or broke up with somebody. She always says she's going to reinvent herself, which mostly means camping out in the guest room and playing show tunes."

"Is that my Pippi?" a voice called from the living room.

Pip widened her eyes at her dad. "You have to tell her she can't call me that," she hissed at him.

He held up his hands placatingly. "Just ride it out, Pip. She'll be on to the next thing before you know it. I have to finish my chapter, or I'll lose my train of thought. The Russians and their idioms, you know how it is. Go entertain your aunt for a bit, will you? I'll be down for dinner." He waved them away and headed for the stairs.

"Welp. Get ready," Pip told Eleanor.

"Gird your loins," Otto suggested.

"Ew," Pip said.

"It just means . . . actually, I don't know what it means," Otto conceded.

"Let's do this." Pip cracked her knuckles, squared her shoulders, and fixed a bright grin on her face. "Auntie Jojo," Pip declared as they entered the living room. "What a surprise!"

Aunt Josephine sat on the couch, a glass filled with something red as a jewel in her hand.

"Pippi!" she declared, leaping to her feet without spilling a drop. Pip marched forward to be squashed.

"It's Pip, Aunt Jojo," she said.

"Right, yes. You're so grown up," Josephine said as she squeezed Pip tight, released her, and then yelped. "Oh my goodness you are soaking wet. And now I am, too." She burst into raucous laughter. "It is positively magnificent to see you. You're taller, aren't you? I told you not to get taller than me." She shook a faux-scolding finger at her niece.

It would have been hard for Pip *not* to get taller than her aunt. Josephine had the same long nose and blonde hair as Pip's dad, but the similarities ended there. Pip's dad was thin and a bit not-quite-there, fading into the background of any gathering, while Josephine seemed like she would fill whatever room she walked into. Everything about this woman seemed big—her voice, her movements, the bright colors she wore, the booming way she laughed at her own jokes. Everything except *her*. She was tiny, barely five feet tall, with a dainty dancer's body.

She'd actually been a ballerina for a while, Pip had said. And then a hair stylist, and then a lawn mower repair technician, and then a welder, and then a florist, and then she'd gotten 37 percent of a PhD in theoretical physics, and then she'd moved to Mexico to be a scuba instructor, and then, most recently, she'd met the love of her life and gone to live with him on his cattle ranch.

Which explained her peacock-blue cowboy boots, but not what she was doing here.

"And Otto, darling," Aunt Josephine said. "Did you get those books I sent you?"

Otto nodded enthusiastically. "They were awesome. I can't wait for the next one to come out. Do you think Captain Dare is really dead?"

"Pshh. They can just upload him into a new clone."

Eleanor hovered awkwardly. No one had introduced her yet, and she didn't want to interrupt. That sort of thing happened a lot. Otto and Pip were so used to knowing everything about each other that they tended to forget that Eleanor didn't.

"HI I'M ELEANOR," she said, way too loud. Why had she done that? Now she was going to have to move to the Yukon and socialize only with moose for the rest of her life.

But Aunt Josephine gave an enthusiastic cry and swept her into a hug, too. "Eleanor! I feel like we're already best friends; I have heard *so* much about you. How are you liking Eden Eld?"

"Oh! Um, it's good?" Eleanor said. Pip and Otto being there was good, at least. The mortal peril bit she was less fond of, but she couldn't tell Josephine that.

Pip cut in. "Aunt Josephine? Not to interrupt, but . . . what are you doing here?" Her father coughed loudly from upstairs. "I mean, to what do we owe this lovely surprise?"

"I thought that would be obvious. I came to help out. Your mother's gone, and Harold is busy with his books. You both need help."

"So what happened to Ranchman McRanchface?" Pip asked. Another cough sounded from upstairs, but this time Pip ignored it.

"Timothy and I were electric. Magnetic. Passionate. Two souls destined for one another," Josephine declared. She lifted her free hand in a flourishing gesture. "For a time."

"You got bored of him?" Pip asked.

"He seemed to think that my fondness for high heels and

lipstick translated into an enthusiasm for doing the vacuuming," Josephine said.

"Yikes," Otto said, wincing.

"I am brilliant at many things. Chores are not among them. But enough about me. Here, let me pour you three some of this deliciousness," Josephine said, gesturing with her glass again.

Pip raised an eyebrow. "You know we're thirteen, right?"

Josephine gave a warm, round chuckle and swanned to the kitchen, which was open to the living room. She opened the fridge and pulled out a tall glass cylinder of red liquid, the same shade as what was in her glass. A white logo was printed on it: six little elongated dots arranged around a cursive double S.

"Six Seed's Patented ImPassion Potion," Josephine said, wiggling the bottle a little as her voice fell into an odd, husky tone. "Packed with antioxidants, vitamins, and toxin-eliminating compounds. All natural, all delicious." She set it on the counter, and her voice returned to normal. "Technically it's a juice cleanse, but I figure if it's tasty, why wait for the cleanse? Drink it now!" She grabbed glasses for the three of them. "Kid-friendly, I promise." She winked.

"I've never heard of it before," Eleanor said.

"It's a SixSeed exclusive product," Aunt Josephine said loftily. "Not carried in stores. I get all sorts of free samples, though, so you're in luck."

"SixSeed?" Eleanor asked, playing with the sounds in her mind. "Like 'succeed'?"

Aunt Josephine flung her hands up in the air, like she was framing words in the sky. "SixSeed! Not just a product line, a lifeline! Tools to transform yourself, your world, your dreams!" She grinned. "They sell essential oils, cleanses, skin-care products, all sorts of stuff. I should say *we* sell. SixSeed is my future. I can feel it."

"Don't try to discourage her," Pip whispered in Eleanor's ear as Aunt Josephine rattled around in the freezer for ice. "She only ever doubles down. That's how we ended up with seven alpacas in our backyard when I was in fourth grade." To her aunt, she said, "That sounds great!"

Right at that moment, something slammed against the front door. They all jumped, Otto giving a loud yelp and nearly knocking over his glass. Pip cast about for the nearest weapon—then the thing at the door started scrabbling at it and barking a very familiar bark.

"What on earth is that?" Josephine asked.

"Just Prince Caspian," Pip said.

"I'll get him," Eleanor offered and trotted to the door. The little dog was throwing himself against the door and barking madly, but when she opened it he bounced away like a rubber ball. He hopped in a tight circle, tail up, growling and barking. For a moment she thought she'd been wrong and it was some other dog, a dull gray-brown instead of Caspian's white with chestnut patches—but she realized he was covered head to toe in thick, gooey mud. And then she saw something else that made her suck in a sharp, alarmed breath.

Caspian's collar was still around his neck, and his leash dangled from it. It trailed on the ground for two feet—and then ended, ragged, as if it had torn.

Or been gnawed through.

Four

"**W**hat's going on?" Pip's dad asked, coming down the stairs.

"It's Mr. Maughan's dog. He must have gotten loose again," Eleanor said. She peered down the driveway, but she couldn't see any sign of Caspian's owner. She swallowed. It didn't mean anything. Maybe the leash had gotten tangled on a branch and Caspian had chewed through it. She'd seen the way he gutted stuffed toys. Those teeth were serious business.

"You kids grab the scamp, and I'll give Mr. Maughan a call," her dad said.

"Come here, pretty puppy," Eleanor cooed, wiggling her fingers. Caspian backed up and barked.

With a chorus of sighs, Eleanor, Otto, and Pip pulled their boots and coats back on and traipsed out. "You go left," Eleanor told Pip. "Otto—"

"The center must hold," he declared, and braced himself in a crouch like a hockey goalie.

Eleanor circled around Caspian. "Come on, Cas," she said. "Let's get you home."

Caspian dodged. He veered toward Otto, changed his mind, and made a mad dash for the trees, but Pip threw herself in a football tackle and rolled, ending on her back with the dog clasped against her chest. "Gotcha, stinker," she said. He flailed and thrashed free, but she had hold of the stub of his leash. When she stood up, she was covered liberally in mud.

"Oh my," Josephine declared, standing within the safety of the doorway with her hand over her heart. "You've taken a turn for the worse since our last encounter, your highness."

"Straight to voicemail," Pip's dad reported from over Josephine's shoulder.

Eleanor's skin went cold, as if it were the dead of winter instead of just chilly, wet March.

Something was wrong. Something was, possibly, capital-W Wrong.

"We can take him over to Mr. Maughan's house," Pip offered. And maybe he would be there, and everything would be fine.

But Eleanor doubted it.

"I'll go with you," Pip's father said.

"You don't have to. We know the way," Otto said.

"We'll be fine," Pip added, and Eleanor nodded vigorously.

He shook his head. "No, I'd better come along. The Russians can wait."

Pip's dad had gotten overprotective since Halloween. He didn't know what had happened—or even that anything *had* happened—but he seemed to sense it. Eleanor caught him looking at Pip sometimes with tears shining in his eyes.

He was one of the other names on the People Definitely Not Involved in the January Society (Revised) list. And Eleanor was happy about that. But sometimes she wished she had a father who would look at her like that, who would worry about her. She didn't have a father at all—not one she knew about, anyway. Her mother hadn't ever given her a name, only promised he was a good man. And yes, she'd tried to find him, and no, Eleanor shouldn't go looking.

Pip kept hold of Caspian while her father got on his coat and shoes. His escape thwarted, Caspian now seemed intent on attacking their feet. If anything had happened to Mr. Maughan, he didn't appear to be worried about it. Then again, he didn't strike Eleanor as a terrifically smart dog.

They tromped out into the rain and down the drive, then turned down the path toward Mr. Maughan's little house. Pip kept the end of Caspian's leash securely wrapped around her fist, and from the way she gripped it, Eleanor could tell she was missing the reassurance of the walking stick. Eleanor scoured the trees for signs of lurking beasts, but nothing leaped out at them or dropped from the dark branches above. They reached the little stone garden path that led to Mr. Maughan's driveway and walked up toward the house.

The front door was wide open, light spilling out into the evening gloom. Mr. Maughan's boots were on the front porch, the mud slowly drying—yet there was mud smearing the floor inside.

Lots and lots of mud.

"Dad," Pip whispered. Caspian growled, ears pricked and eyes fixed on the house.

"Stay here," Pip's dad said, sounding troubled, but when he strode toward the house, they all followed close behind. He didn't know about the Wrong Things. He could be walking into something he couldn't even see, much less protect himself from.

"Mr. Maughan?" Eleanor called.

"Mathew?" Pip's dad called.

Neither of them got an answer. They crept in cautiously, none of them bothering to remove their boots. It wasn't as if they could make the entryway any dirtier. Mud was smeared everywhere. Some of the splotches might have been footprints, but elsewhere it seemed to have splattered onto the ground, or been swirled around like finger paint. It covered the walls, too, and in the center of the wall to the right of the door was a single muddy handprint, smeared as if its owner had been pulled—*dragged*—away.

"Goodness," Pip's dad said. His eyes seemed almost glazed

over. "Bit of a mess, isn't it? But that's bachelors for you. Mathew, are you here?" He walked forward leadenly, and Eleanor and the others stared at him. He didn't seem nearly as alarmed as he should be. Which meant one kind of thing was happening—the *Wrong* kind. Most people couldn't see them, or didn't understand what they saw. Especially adults.

Pip stuck close to her dad as they walked into the interior of the house, Eleanor and Otto trailing behind and fanning out once they got past the entryway. There was no mud past the foyer—and no sign of Mr. Maughan.

"Well. I suppose he might be out looking for the dog," Pip's dad mused.

"Barefoot?" Otto muttered.

Pip's dad scratched his head. "I guess we could leave the dog here for him."

"No," all three of them said immediately, in unison. Pip cleared her throat. "We should take him home with us. He'd get the whole house muddy."

"He can't stay with us, dear, I'm allergic," her father reminded her.

"If I bring another animal home, my mom will flip," Otto said.

"I'll take him. We've got the room," Eleanor said.

"Okay," Pip said reluctantly and Eleanor took Caspian from her. Ben and Jenny wouldn't say no. They had about a million empty rooms, and besides, her aunt and uncle tried very hard not to disappoint her these days, given her enormous amounts of trauma and all.

Prince Caspian huddled against her as they walked back. The tension seemed to have gone out of him, and Eleanor wondered if he had been hoping to find Mr. Maughan, too. All the way back, she searched for any sign of Mr. Maughan's green jacket or his argyle sweater. But there was only darkness, and the steady squelch of mud beneath their feet.

After she was home, tucked into bed with Caspian snoring beside her, she waited for her phone to buzz with a text from Pip, saying it had been a mistake. Mr. Maughan had come back. He was fine. Mr. January was just messing with them. But her phone stayed silent.

It didn't stop raining until morning.

Five

Eleanor didn't know when she finally fell asleep, only that she woke with Caspian burrowed into the blankets next to her, smelling of dog and of the baby shampoo they'd used to gently wash the mud off him. As soon as she stirred, he bolted to his feet and started whining again, his ears pinned back to his skull and then popping forward to focus on her.

"You want to go find your dad, huh?" she asked him. She checked the time. Barely five. She probably shouldn't—

Her phone vibrated. Otto, on their group chat.

Anybody up?

Turned out none of them were sleeping well. In a few minutes they had a plan and a place to meet. After she'd let him outside to do his business, Eleanor put Caspian in the room Uncle Ben had helped set up for him—he'd even made an emergency run to the store for chew toys—and patted him on the head. "We'll get your dad," she promised.

He farted. And then barked at the fart. Eleanor sighed. "You're lucky you're cute."

She dressed quickly and warmly and triple-checked her supplies. *Thirteen Tales of the Gray* was with Pip, but she packed protein bars, water bottles, a change of socks, and a folded-up map of Eden Eld. She left a note for Jenny and Ben and went to get her bike.

She met up with Otto on the way. He lived just down the road from her, near the edge of Eden Eld. This far from the town center, the magic that kept everything perfect was a little weaker, and there were a few storm-downed trees and random bits of trash near the road, but as they got farther in, things grew more orderly. Even the trees were spaced just so, a kind of random that didn't seem random at all.

They stowed their bikes at Pip's house. The paths were so muddy they'd had to walk them the last bit anyway. With flashlights in hand and only a few tense, muttered words of greeting out of the way, they started toward Mr. Maughan's house.

The rain had left the path a muddy ribbon through the trees. If there had been footprints or signs of a struggle, they were long since washed away. The wind whistled and moaned, and the branches *tap-tap-tapp*ed in a strange, steady rhythm. They got all the way to Mr. Maughan's house without finding any sign of him, or of what had happened.

The mud in the foyer had dried to a light gray, so colorless that it made Eleanor shiver with the memory of Mr. January's world. "What now?" Eleanor asked.

"I guess we look around," Pip said, already walking in. Eleanor envied Pip that ability to just do things, instead of over-thinking and second-guessing and needing plans and backup plans and backup backup plans before she could get anything done.

In the living room, a single armchair sat opposite a television. A clock ticked somewhere in the house, but otherwise it was si-lent. The TV was blocked by piles and piles of books that didn't fit on the three bookshelves against the wall, and more were stacked beside the chair, several with improvised bookmarks stuck into them—pens, receipts, the TV remote. Eleanor peered at the titles. Mr. Maughan had eclectic taste—everything from chemistry books to Greek myths to *The Mycology Encyclopedia*.

"It doesn't seem like whoever grabbed Mr. Maughan went farther into the house," Otto said, crouching to peer at the car-pet. "No more mud. Except the stuff we're bringing in."

Eleanor lifted her crystal to her eye to double-check, but everything looked the same through it as without it. She went back to the foyer, but it was the same there—no difference with the crystal. She could make out human footprints here and there. And then there were the big paintbrush strokes of mud, like something had been dragged or swiped around. And the handprint, which looked like Mr. Maughan's, too.

She turned around in a slow circle—and gasped. Last night they'd left the door open, which meant they hadn't seen what was on the other side: deep claw marks that raked across it. There were five furrows—like a five-fingered hand had made them. The marks were arranged in a pattern. One long set down the middle of the door, almost top to bottom. A shorter set slashed from left to right, cutting the big line in half, and then two more sets, each one shorter than the last, were below that. The effect was almost like an upside-down pine tree.

"Holy cow," Otto breathed.

An unsettling sense of familiarity crept over Eleanor. She'd seen that before, hadn't she? "Pip," she said. "Did you bring *Thirteen Tales*?"

"Yeah. I tried to read some of it last night," Pip said. She looked a little embarrassed. "I didn't exactly get very far."

"That's okay," Eleanor said. Pip wasn't a fast reader. Her mind always wandered, and she'd end up on her phone watching YouTube tutorials about how to pick locks, or doodling knights fighting dragons in her notebook. "I think I know which story this is from, that's all."

Pip nodded and dug *Thirteen Tales of the Gray* out of her backpack.

Eleanor flipped through, scanning the pages that had illustrations. The book had gone back to having only twelve stories in it. The thirteenth tale had appeared only on Halloween, and the next time they thought to check it, it had vanished again. Luckily, what she was looking for was in one of the middle stories, "Brackenbeast." One of the Jack stories.

In the forest outside the village of Wick, it began, *there lurked a terrible beast.*

She knew all the stories by heart, but she had to admit this one wasn't her favorite. The beast was kidnapping children. When it carried them off into the woods, they were never seen again. Jack and his friend, a woman who was only ever called the hedgewitch, came to Wick and heard about their troubles. That night they waited, hidden outside one of the houses, and when the brackenbeast came for the boy inside, they followed it into the woods, and then through "a strange sort of passage" to its lair. There they found all of the stolen children. *The children were asleep,* the story said, *so still and so cold they were almost dead.*

The hedgewitch managed to wake them, but then the brackenbeast returned. Jack fought with Gloaming, his magical sword. The monster tore the sword from his hands and flung it away into the woods. Jack picked up a strong, straight stick from the forest floor and used it to hold the beast off, but then he had to retreat. The story ended with everyone celebrating, and Jack swearing to go back to reclaim Gloaming one day. But he hadn't, as far as Eleanor knew. In all the rest of the stories, he carried not a sword but his walking stick.

Eleanor was remembering why she hadn't paid as much attention to this story as to the others. There were bits that didn't get explained—like how they had known which of the houses the brackenbeast was coming to. Or what the brackenbeast even looked like. Or what the passage to its lair was.

There were only two illustrations. The first one didn't seem to have anything important in it. It showed Jack and the hedgewitch arriving in Wick. As usual, the two heroes were shown from behind, standing at the edge of a town square. It was full of kids, and they seemed to be doing some kind of egg hunt, like on Easter.

It was the second illustration that Eleanor was most interested in. It showed Jack carrying Gloaming, which seemed to blaze with light, leading the hedgewitch through what might have been a tunnel or just darkness, vague scratchy lines marking out shadows around them. In front of them was a rough door, maybe made of stone. And on it was scratched a symbol made of four lines, one vertical and three horizontal, that looked almost like an upside-down tree.

"That there is what we call a clue," Otto said, tapping the page as he leaned over Eleanor's shoulder.

"So a brackenbeast took Mr. Maughan," Eleanor said. "Whatever a brackenbeast is."

Pip was staring at the illustration in the book, chewing on her bottom lip.

"Something wrong?" Eleanor asked.

"It's nothing," Pip said.

"Come on. What is it?" Eleanor pressed.

But Pip waved a hand. "Ignore me. You guys are the figure-outers. I'm just here to whack stuff. Let me know when the monsters show up."

Eleanor decided to let it drop and turned the page. The next story, "The Kindly Dark," had Jack in it, too. But he was more of a supporting character, with most of the tale being about the girl with backward hands—and it didn't mention anything about the town of Wick or the brackenbeast or the strange symbol.

"Hold on," Otto said. "Go back?"

Eleanor obeyed, flipping back to the page with the illustration of the egg hunt.

"Look at this," Otto said. He pointed at the sky behind the children. It was divided neatly in half: one side for night, one side for day. The sun and moon were joined in the middle so that each of them made up half of a single circle.

"What's that supposed to represent?" Eleanor asked.

"Day and night are equal. The day and night are exactly the same length on the spring equinox," Otto said, excitement in his voice. "Mr. January said that each of them have their season. Mr. January could only come after us on Halloween. His sister has to have a different day."

"When is the spring equinox?" Eleanor asked, silently hoping the answer was at least a few weeks away.

"It's . . . um. It's on Saturday," Otto said, blood draining from his face.

"Today is Wednesday," Pip said. "That's too soon! We're not ready!"

"Look on the bright side. Last time we didn't figure this stuff out until the day before Halloween. We have way more time now," Otto said, but his cheer was forced.

"Four days isn't much," Eleanor said weakly.

"We should go back out," Pip said. "We kind of know what we're looking for now. Maybe we'll spot something we missed."

"Maybe we should read the story again," Eleanor said.

"Elle, if you haven't found anything in it yet, you're not going to find it now," Pip said, impatient, and started out the door. Eleanor's cheeks were hot as she shoved the book into her bag and followed Pip out.

The sun had risen higher since they'd gone inside, and now she could see the area in front of the house more clearly. There was a bit of lawn, a small garden, and a flagstone path leading to the driveway. Not a blade of grass bent out of place. Except . . .

"Look. The mud's a different color," Otto said, pointing. Globs of the same grayish mud that coated the hall and had turned Caspian into a mud prince led toward the trees.

They followed the path across the lawn and into the trees. Water dripped steadily from the branches around them.

They only made it twenty feet into the woods before the trail petered out. Whatever mud the kidnapper—the brackenbeast?—had left behind had vanished amid the general muddiness of the forest. Eleanor halted, frustrated and relieved all at once.

And then she saw it: a bit of blue. She lurched toward it with a cry.

"What is it?" Pip asked.

The leash dangled from a branch that grew low to the ground. The ragged end of the leash hung in the air, the fluffy bits of nylon where it had been bitten through fluttering in the breeze. The other end fell all the way to the ground. The hand loop was half-sunk in a patch of extra-thick mud.

Eleanor touched the end of it and looked at the others. "Caspian must have gotten stuck and chewed through it," she said.

Pip squelched past her to peer at the mud patch, then grabbed a stick from the ground and used it to lift the leash free. It flopped onto the ground. She prodded at the mud. The stick sank in—and kept sinking for six inches before Pip pulled it back. It came out with a wet sucking sound that made Eleanor's skin crawl.

"Did Mr. Maughan fall into the mud?" Pip asked.

"Mud isn't quicksand," Otto objected. "It wouldn't just suck you in."

Pip stepped closer. "Careful," Eleanor said. Pip gave her an annoyed look.

"Careful, careful, careful. If we were as careful as you want us to be, we'd just hide in our beds and never get anything done," Pip complained.

"And you think 'plan' is a kind of dessert," Otto said teasingly, poking her arm. Eleanor smiled, but it was the lying kind of smile she was so good at. It seemed like no matter what she did, all she could do these days was annoy Pip.

Pip thought she was too careful? Fine. Eleanor strode forward to the mud pit, pushing past Pip, and dropped into a crouch. It was maybe three feet across, and sunken a bit in the middle. All along the edges, little black mushrooms grew, their delicate caps wrinkled and withered. Just mud. Nothing scary about mud. She shoved her sleeve up to her elbow and reached for the pit before anyone—including herself—could stop her.

Her fingertips sank readily into the mud. It was thick and slimy and cold. There were no stones, no bits of bark or branches, just silty mud that her hand plunged through without resistance. She pushed it in up to the wrist, then up to the middle of her arm, kneeling with her hand braced against the ground. There had to be a bottom to it, didn't there?

Her hand bumped against something, and she gave a little yelp—then grabbed hold of it. She drew the object out and shook the grime from it.

It was Mr. Maughan's glasses.

Six

Her breath hissed out between her teeth. "That's not a good sign," she said.

"Do you think he drowned in there?" Otto asked, sounding queasy.

Eleanor didn't want to think Mr. Maughan was dead. In the story, the kids were rescued—but the stories weren't true, exactly. They were full of hints and truths told slyly, sideways. You had to puzzle them out and see the connections.

"What's *that*?" Otto exclaimed. He walked over and dropped to one knee next to the base of a tree, a few feet from the mud pit. "Whoa. It's a glimmermander. I think."

It wasn't a shining, shimmering creature. This salamander was black. Its tail was curled up over its face, its limbs tucked tightly under. It had made itself into a ball, its eyes squeezed shut.

"Is it even alive?" Eleanor asked.

Otto touched its side gently. "It feels cold, but it's breathing. Maybe it's hibernating," he suggested.

"You should probably leave it alone," Pip said. Nothing they'd met from the gray world, or any of the Wrong Things, had been sweet and nice. Even the cat-of-ashes had bitten Eleanor so hard she still had a scar, a semicircle of tooth-marks that sat neatly within the crescent burn that already marked her palm. Ignoring Pip's warning, Otto lifted the salamander carefully, cradling it in his palms. He loved animals. His father was a vet, and Otto helped him rehabilitate all kinds of injured wildlife.

"We should keep one to study it," Otto said. "We released Fiddlesticks last week, so I have a spare terrarium at home."

"Fiddlesticks was the . . . duck?" Pip asked.

"No, that's Maleficent, and she's still recovering. Fiddlesticks is a turtle," Otto said. "Hit by a car? Fractured shell?"

"Right, I remember," Pip said unconvincingly.

"Here. You can put it in my lunch box," Eleanor said. They tucked the salamander into the lunch box and nestled the lunch-box into Eleanor's backpack. "Class is going to start soon. We should probably head back," Eleanor said when they were done.

"We could skip," Pip suggested.

"Not all of us are the headmistress's daughter," Eleanor said, and regretted it immediately. Pip made a sour face. Everyone in town seemed to have decided that Delilah Foster was on a European sabbatical, studying in Austria or Spain or sometimes Greece, depending on who you talked to. The only people who knew the truth—that she'd been sucked into the gray world Mr. January came from—were the kids and whatever members the January Society had left. The school had an interim headmaster, a bland man who didn't *seem* evil (unless he was secretly killing them all through sheer boredom), but Pip still got treated like her mom's daughter first, and her own person second. Which was hard enough when your mom *wasn't* evil.

"You're right," was all Pip said, though, and Eleanor was relieved. She didn't want Pip mad at her. She wanted to be friends the way they were on Halloween. But Pip wasn't getting less angry, she was getting worse. And Eleanor was getting worse at helping her.

Feeling defeated, they trudged through the trees toward school.

THE SCHOOL DAY passed in a blur as sodden and miserable as the weather. Every minute felt like time wasted, but they'd lose more time if they got caught skipping and ended up grounded. By the time the final bell rang, Eleanor was ready to dive out her classroom window to escape. She raced to the back of the school building, where Pip and Otto met her a few seconds later.

Since Pip's house was close to Mr. Maughan's, and since Uncle Ben had texted to let Eleanor know he and Caspian were having "guy time" and not to worry about the pup, they decided to head over that way. Pip and Otto walked out in front, chatting. Eleanor tried to keep up with the conversation, but they were in one of those modes where they only said half sentences or mentioned "that time when . . ." and then lurched to the next subject without explaining. It wasn't their fault, and she didn't want to make them feel bad. So she just walked by herself.

And, yeah, moped a little. Sometimes moping felt good. Good in the way cold, gooey mud felt good squishing between your fingers.

Sometimes she felt like she didn't really belong to anyone. Aunt Jenny and Uncle Ben had the new baby, and as great as they were, Eleanor wasn't really their daughter. She was just a girl who lived in their house. She looked at the way they held little Naomi, sang to her and rocked her, and she wished she could be theirs—and just as fiercely wished she had her mother back, that she even knew who her father was. But her father was a mystery, and her mother was gone. Every day her memory got a little harder to hold on to.

"Is your dad having a party or something?" Otto asked Pip as they approached the house.

Eleanor looked up, curious. The driveway had sprouted more cars—not just Pip's dad's and Aunt Josephine's, but a blue Honda, a maroon SUV that had those stick figure stickers on the back window, and a sleek silver convertible with the top up. "Dad doesn't have parties. They must be here for Aunt Josephine," Pip said.

When Pip opened the door, a wash of scent rolled out. Otto

sneezed. Eleanor made a little gurgling noise and covered her nose. It wasn't that it was a bad smell—it was just *so much*. Sweet and fruity and floral and spicy, rolled together and then rolled again. It made Eleanor's eyes water.

They ditched their coats and boots and headed into the living room, exchanging bewildered glances.

Four women were sitting around the room. Aunt Josephine sat in the middle of the couch, the center of attention as she told a story involving an untamed horse and her ex-boyfriend. Perched on a chair nearby was a narrow-faced woman Eleanor recognized vaguely. Susannah Chen, who had worked for Pip's dentist until he turned out to be evil, was in the armchair, clutching a glass of purple juice and looking like she was trying not to laugh. A fourth woman sat demurely on a dining chair that had been brought into the room, her ankles crossed, her own drink held delicately cradled in both hands.

SixSeed-branded boxes and products were piled high on the coffee table and scattered around the room. Eleanor's eyes roved over the stack, trying to pick out the product names, but the sheer quantity was overwhelming. SixSeed Hand of Fortune Hand Cream. SixSeed TruHarmony Essential Oil Diffuser. SixSeed ReJubilation Mushroom-Boosted Mud Mask. SixSeed Red as Red Lipstick. There was even a SixSeed Super Storage Solution for holding all your SixSeed solutions.

Aunt Josephine had wrapped up her story, and her guests were wiping their eyes and chortling, when they all noticed the kids.

"Oh, Pippi. I mean, Pip-just-Pip," Aunt Josephine said. "Don't mind us! We're just having a little get-together."

"They sell SixSeed stuff, too?" Pip guessed.

"Yes, isn't it wonderful? Susannah has been a SixSeed representative for *years*, and she's agreed to help show June and me the ropes," Josephine said. She flourished a hand toward the fourth woman, the one sitting on the dining room chair. "This is Korri Prosper. She's the regional sales representative for the entire county!"

"Oh," Pip managed.

"Coooool," Otto intoned.

"Neat," Eleanor supplied, suffusing it with sincerity. Adults were easier to fool than other kids, but Korri Prosper gave her a knowing look all the same.

"We're planning a SixSeed party," Aunt Josephine said. "Free samples and special discounts for all! You should invite your mom, Otto."

"Okay, but does SixSeed cater to a range of skin tones? Because if you've just got one foundation called, like, Mocha, you're gonna get a really long email," Otto said warningly.

"SixSeed caters to all who yearn for transformation," Korri Prosper said. Her voice was soft and musical. A smile creased her lips. "And we make sure that our designers reflect the diversity of our clients. Here."

She reached over to the coffee table with a fluid movement and held out a brochure to Otto. It showed an image of six people arranged like color swatches, from a milky-skinned redhead at one end, dabbing concealer onto her cheek, to a bronze-skinned man wearing iridescent eye shadow, to a dark-skinned woman applying a shock of bright purple lipstick.

"And do you test on animals or—"

"Only the human kind. All our products are vegan and cruelty-free," she said, and her smile spread a little more. "It's all in the brochure, or I'm happy to give you the whole speech."

"That's all right," Pip said quickly. Eleanor couldn't think of a topic Pip would be *less* enthusiastic about sitting through a lecture on. She'd once confided that her mother was always trying to get her to wear makeup. Cover up her "aggressive" freckles, put on a bit of mascara to "deal with those invisible eyelashes of yours," wear a bit of lipstick "so your mouth doesn't look so thin."

But Eleanor eyed the stack of products with curiosity. Her mom loved makeup. She'd delighted in trying out different looks, making her eyelids sparkle with gold or gleaming green, coating her lips with ruby red or plummy purple. Some of Eleanor's favorite memories were of playing "night out" together, getting fancied up and then putting on pajamas and watching old movies.

There weren't a lot of good times, so the ones she'd had, she treasured.

"We should go upstairs," Pip said pointedly. "We've got homework." She widened her eyes at the others.

"Right," Eleanor said, a little disappointed.

"Nice to meet you," Otto added, but Pip was already heading up the stairs, and they had to scramble to follow.

As soon as they reached Pip's room, Otto unzipped Eleanor's backpack to check on the salamander, and Eleanor and Pip waited patiently. The rain must have started again, because there was a steady *tap-tap-tap* against the window.

"He's okay," Otto declared after a careful examination. "Or she. Or they? I don't know how to tell on a salamander. I should look it up. Though it might not be the same for a *magical* salamander, so . . ."

He kept talking, but Eleanor just let his words wash over her, staring at the window as she thought. "Why is 'Brackenbeast' so short and so vague?" Eleanor wondered when he'd wound down. *Thirteen Tales* had been written by Bartimaeus Ashford, one of the founders of Eden Eld. He'd made the original deal with Mr. January to let him turn Eden Eld's kids into keys, but he'd also helped them escape the curse by leaving clues in the stories, among other things. He'd even built Ashford House, where Eleanor lived. They'd met him briefly on Halloween—he was nearly two hundred years old, but he'd hidden himself away in a secret, magical room that kept him alive.

"It's like Bartimaeus was trying to write it after hearing half a story," Pip suggested, and Eleanor nodded. "All the stuff about Mr. January was stuff he knew himself. But none of the stories have as much to say about Mr. January's sisters."

"It's almost like he only thought the dude was a threat, and the girls were just sidekicks," Eleanor said dryly.

"Not like that's ever happened before," Pip replied, and both of them rolled their eyes while Otto chuckled. Eleanor tucked her smile down deep, but she felt warm all over. Maybe things were getting better with Pip.

"I wish we knew what that symbol meant," she said.

"I wish we had more to go off of than one not-that-helpful book," Pip replied. Then she frowned, like she was remembering something.

"What is it?" Eleanor asked.

But once again, Pip only shook her head. "Nothing," she said.

Eleanor's phone chimed with a calendar reminder. She groaned. "Dang it. I have to go soon. I have my thing." She went to a therapist on Wednesdays. It was at Jenny and Ben's insistence, but she couldn't really argue that she didn't need therapy.

"Right. How's that going?" Pip asked.

"Okay, I guess. Dr. Lillian's nice, but she thinks I'm avoiding talking about things. Which I am, because it's not like I can explain that a talking cat told me my mom's out there somewhere and didn't actually try to kill me." Eleanor shrugged.

"Yeah, it's like that for me, too," Pip said. Eleanor felt something shift in her chest, like a little bit of pressure easing off her. "We can talk about my 'abandonment issues,' but my therapist thinks I just mean that I'm mad my mom went off to Europe or whatever. And not that she *did* try to kill me."

"Maybe if we disguised ourselves as each other we could get closer to talking about the real issues," Eleanor said.

"Easy," Otto said. "Give Pip your glasses, and I'll draw freckles on you. And you'll both need wigs."

"I have always wanted to have red hair," Eleanor said. Pip looked skeptical. "No, really. When I was five I cried because I didn't."

"Okay, but it comes with getting sunburned in fifteen minutes on a cloudy day," Pip warned her.

"Fair trade for smudgy glasses," Eleanor countered. "And when it rains and you get raindrops all over the lenses? The worst."

"I see no potential flaws in this plan," Otto declared. They all grinned at each other.

But Pip wasn't as good at faking a smile as Eleanor was. And Eleanor could see the truth beneath: the anger that was always there, simmering and snapping.

Pip wasn't okay. And neither was Eleanor. And neither was Otto, for that matter—his parents might be great, but that didn't make him any less cursed. They were all faking it.

And Eleanor couldn't help but feel that soon it was all going to fall apart.

Seven

Aunt Jenny arrived a half hour later. Otto lived in the same direction, so she offered to give him a ride, too. Pip and the others were saying their goodbyes when Aunt Josephine came into the entryway, smiling ear to ear.

"You must be this Jenny I've heard so much about," she said.

"Oh?" Jenny replied, clearly taken aback. "I'm sorry, I—"

"Have no idea who I am," Aunt Josephine finished for her. She stuck out her hand. "Josephine. Pip's favorite aunt. And least favorite, come to think of it, since I'm the only one!"

It was almost funny, seeing the two of them shaking hands. Aunt Josephine wore a drapey shawl that shimmered in pinks and purples, and she had giant hoop earrings and big chunky rings on all of her fingers. Aunt Jenny wore a black tank top and a comfy gray sweater and jeans with holes in the knees. She kept her curly hair back in a ponytail and Eleanor had never seen her wear makeup.

Aunt Josephine touched Jenny lightly on the shoulder. "You *must* come to this little get-together we're planning for Friday. Just a few girls and a few gifts and no pressure whatsoever. Like a spa day and a cocktail hour all swirled together."

"That sounds like fun," Jenny said doubtfully.

"Wonderful. I'll be in touch, then!" Aunt Josephine declared. "Oh! You need a sample bag. Eleanor, be a dear and go grab one for your aunt?"

"Sure," Eleanor said, and ducked into the living room. Pip went with her, but Otto had already pulled on his boots and so he waited by the door. Susannah and June had left, but the regional whatever-she-was stood packing up her things, tucking each bottle and box into a big silver suitcase. "I'm supposed to get a sample bag?" Eleanor said hesitantly.

"Of course, dear," the woman said, holding out a purple gift bag. Her voice had this melodious quality to it that made Eleanor think of a cold, rolling stream. Eleanor took it with a grateful nod. Their fingers brushed against each other briefly. The woman's skin was as cool and as smooth as her voice.

"Thanks—sorry, I forgot your name."

"Mrs. Prosper," she replied. "Or Korri, though I'll be honest, I'm a bit old-fashioned. I prefer the more formal option. And what about you, Pip? Would you like a bag?"

"I hate makeup," Pip said flatly.

Mrs. Prosper laughed, unbothered. "It isn't just makeup. We have lotions, creams . . . Whatever your heart's desire. You'd honestly be helping me by taking them off my hands. I've got to pack everything up, and you know how it is. Once you let everything out of the box it's somehow impossible to get it back in again."

"No, really, it's fine," Pip said.

"Tell me. Why do you hate makeup?" Mrs. Prosper asked.

Pip gave an uncomfortable shrug. "I guess because it's so fake," Pip said. "I don't like hiding who I am."

"Interesting," Mrs. Prosper replied. "And can people tell who you are just by looking at you?"

"I—no," Pip said, stammering a little.

"Makeup has a lot of uses. It can help hide imperfections. It can help create a false impression, certainly. Or it can give you a way to show the world who you truly are. It can be a mask. Or battle paint. Or a bit of beauty. It's a way to tell a story, and only you can decide whether it's truth or fiction. You don't have to wear makeup if you don't want to—but don't dismiss people who do."

"I guess that makes sense," Pip said. "It's just, my mom was always telling me I should wear it."

"Why was that?" Mrs. Prosper asked, her head cocked, eyes sharp with interest.

"Um. My eyelashes are too pale, and I have too many freckles, that sort of thing," Pip said.

"Do you like the way you look with darker eyelashes?"

"Not really?" Pip said.

"Definitely skip the mascara, then," Mrs. Prosper replied, and winked. "My mother was controlling, too. But she would never have let me wear makeup. She didn't want me to grow up too fast. She kept me sheltered from the world, but that only meant I didn't know how to protect myself. There are so many ways that mothers can make mistakes, sometimes it's a marvel to me that there are some who manage the job at all."

Eleanor couldn't argue with that. "I'd better go," she said to Pip. "I'll see you tomorrow, okay?"

Pip nodded, and they hugged. It was a brief, awkward little squeeze, and Eleanor had a moment of panic. What if she was wrong? What if they *weren't* friends? She liked makeup—did Pip think she was fake?

Maybe they'd only fooled themselves into thinking they were friends because they were in danger together.

Mrs. Prosper snapped the suitcase shut. She pulled out the handle and started rolling it toward the door. "Can I walk you out, dear?" she asked Eleanor. Eleanor nodded, glad for the excuse to just leave before she could freak herself out any more.

As she walked beside Mrs. Prosper, she caught a whiff of a faint floral scent, and something cool and damp like stone. Almost to the door, Mrs. Prosper paused.

"It was lovely to meet you properly, Eleanor," she said. "I look forward to seeing you again soon. You, and Pip, and Otto." She smiled, and this smile had teeth. "Tick tock."

Eleanor felt rooted to the spot. She stared, shock and horror paralyzing her, as Mrs. Prosper walked out the door and out of sight. They'd tracked mud into the house when they came in.

Mrs. Prosper's heels left backward footprints where she walked.

The door opened, and then it shut.

Tick tock.

The words echoed in Eleanor's mind—and then they transformed. Not words at all, but the sound she'd been hearing since yesterday. When she was riding home from Pip's she'd thought it was the drumming of the rain. And then she'd thought it was the clacking of tree branches in the wind. And then she'd gotten closer, in Mr. Maughan's house.

Tick tock tick.

It was the ticking of a clock—a very particular clock. It was a clock that stood in the hall outside Eleanor's room. A clock that ran backward. A clock that she'd last heard tick-tock-ticking away on Halloween, the day Mr. January came for them. And it was getting louder.

Eight

SHE'S HER, Eleanor texted frantically, running toward the door.

??? came the reply from Otto. He was already standing by Jenny's car while Aunt Josephine regaled Jenny with some story. Mrs. Prosper made her way across the driveway to her sleek convertible and loaded the suitcase into it, casual as anything.

Korri Prosper is one of the People Who Look Away, she stabbed out, watching with every muscle tensed as Mrs. Prosper slid into the driver's seat of the car.

Her phone buzzed. *????????????* sent Otto, and *wait, what?* from Pip, and then she looked at what she'd actually sent.

korfu ootkser ibd r of dvhe peoeehe look anyway

Autocorrect had taken its best guess at the last words but given up on the rest, apparently. Her hands were shaking too much to type, so she thumbed the voice-to-text button and hissed into the phone. "Mrs. Prosper is one of the People Who Look Away!"

!!!!!!!!

"Where is she?" Pip demanded, bursting in from the back room.

Eleanor pointed. She thumbed the voice-to-text back on so she could message Otto while she explained to Pip. "She pretty much told me what she was, though. She said she'd see us all soon. And I can hear the clock."

I hear it too, Otto texted, just as Pip said the same thing. *I didn't notice it until just now.*

The clock ticking faintly in the distance had been built by Bartimaeus Ashford—the same man who'd built Eleanor's house, who'd written the *Thirteen Tales*, and who had signed the original deal that put Eden Eld in the grip of the People Who Look Away.

Safe? Otto asked.

He meant, are we safe? And were they? Mrs. Prosper was pulling out of the driveway. Her threat hadn't been immediate. The People Who Look Away tricked you, trapped you. Made you play their games. They didn't just want to win. They wanted to watch you struggle. To hope—and then to lose all hope.

For now, I think, Eleanor texted back. Jenny was waving at her to hurry. She tucked the phone in her back pocket.

"Be careful," Eleanor told Pip. For once, Pip didn't roll her eyes.

"I can promise you one thing. If she's tricking us with makeup, she seriously miscalculated. There was already no way I was going to touch that stuff."

"Good," Eleanor said. "Are you sure you're going to be okay alone here?"

"Just go," Pip said. "I'll be fine."

"Eleanor! Come on, we're going to be late!" Jenny called.

Eleanor made her way to the car. As she got in, her phone buzzed. She looked down to see a text from Pip.

You be careful too, it said.

From the doorway, Pip lifted a hand in farewell.

There were two more days till the equinox.

IT WAS A grotesque fact of their lives that no matter how dire the circumstance, they had to go to school. It was a point of pride at Eden Eld Academy that the school had never been closed on a school day—not for bad weather or anything else—except for one snow day every year, on January 14 (or the following Monday). They acted like it was because of how awesome the Academy was, but Eleanor knew it had more to do with their ancestors making an evil bargain with Mr. January a hundred-odd years ago.

Eden Eld Academy kept to its schedule and never faltered. Eleanor was not so lucky today.

No, today she was late because Caspian had escaped his room, jetted down the hall, and declared war on the toilet paper. By the time she'd secured him and made sure everything he could possibly chew on—and hadn't destroyed already—was locked in the closet, she'd missed the bus, which meant Jenny had to load baby Naomi, wailing and shaking her pudgy fist, into the car and give Eleanor a ride. She sprinted across campus but still arrived seven minutes late for first period.

She slinked in and hustled to her seat near the back of the room. The teacher gave her a surprised look. "Everything all right, Miss Barton?"

"Fine," she panted. Five months of good grades and near-perfect attendance had apparently won her a single instance of forgiveness, because that was all that he said on the matter.

Eleanor's seatmate, April Berry, gave her a disdainful look and leaned over to Mabel Cox, her best friend, who sat at the next table over.

"You should *totally* come over. Seriously. Travis will be *completely* into you. He won't be able to help it. Not when you're like a shimmery dewy goddess of perfection."

Mabel Cox was always a shimmery dewy goddess of perfection, Eleanor thought to herself. She had doe-like brown eyes and glossy mahogany hair that tumbled down to her shoulders in effortless waves. Otto thought Mabel had the personality of a damp paper towel, but that might have had something to do with how she'd edged him out for first prize at the science fair four years running.

"Your skin looks *amazing* right now, for sure," Mabel gushed. "We should do an unboxing video."

"*Totally,*" April agreed. "We could be, like, *influencers.*" She swiped on a thick layer of bubblegum-pink lip gloss. Guys had started falling all over themselves about April, but Eleanor didn't see what was so incredible about her other than the fact that she was blonde, which as Otto pointed out only meant she'd inherited a recessive gene. Big whoop. The fact that Mabel liked both her and Travis, a boy in search of a single, solitary opinion to hold, was the main strike against her.

Eleanor caught a glimpse of the logo stamped on the bottom of the tube of lip gloss. SixSeed.

"Your mom's name is June, isn't it?" Eleanor asked.

April's head rotated like an owl's to stare at her. "Yes?" she said, managing to sound both bored and affronted. "April and June. And no, I don't have a sister named May."

"No, I just—I met her yesterday, that's all," Eleanor said.

"O-kaaaay," April intoned. She turned back to Mabel. "Ugh. Anyway." Mabel caught Eleanor's eyes over April's back and gave a little one-shoulder shrug.

SixSeed. The name plucked at something in Eleanor's memory. The January Society had named itself—and the man they served—after Janus, the Greek god with two faces. Because the People Who Look Away were two-faced, in a way, looking away and at you at the same time.

Six seeds. Six seeds. Where did she know that from?

She needed to ask Pip. Pip knew all the Greek gods—her dad had told her the myths growing up.

Class stole her focus from there on, and she was still pondering the question when lunchtime rolled around and she finally got to dart out to the courtyard where she and Otto and Pip always met up. Otto was already there, sitting on a low brick wall and staring down at his phone.

"He's still not moving," he informed her as she approached.

"Who?" she asked.

"Kevin," he said.

"I'm sorry, *who*?" Pip asked, appearing from the other direction.

"Oh! The glimmermander. I set up a webcam so I could keep an eye on him," Otto explained, holding the phone out so they could see the grainy image of what looked like a black rock in a fish tank. They stared for a weirdly long time in complete silence before they realized what they were doing and straightened up. Eleanor and Pip took seats on either side of Otto.

"That clock is getting really annoying," Pip said.

Eleanor nodded. It had been there all night and all day. *Tick-tock-tick*. Incessant. Sometimes she almost managed to forget it was there, but never quite. It never let her relax, and tension had been gathering around her shoulders all day.

"Last time it started ticking when Mr. January arrived in Eden Eld. And this time, it started ticking when Mrs. Prosper did," Pip said.

"Plausible," Otto replied.

"More than plausible," Pip said. "I'm sure of it."

"The scientific method—"

"Come on, Otto. We don't have time for experiments and conclusions and reformulated hypotheses. It's time to stop *talking* and do something about it."

Eleanor swung her backpack off and set it on the wall beside her. "I was thinking. Maybe we can do better than reading Bartimaeus's book. Maybe we can find Bartimaeus. If he could fill in some of the gaps in 'Brackenbeast' . . . "

Pip's cheeks went red, and the anger in her eyes was more intense than Eleanor had ever seen it. "Bartimaeus. As in the man who looked right in our eyes when we were scared and running for our lives, and said he'd done enough? Right. Let's find Bartimaeus—except wait. He's a giant coward who's disappeared without a trace." She snapped her fingers. "Or we could ask the cat-of-ashes! Except she's gone, too. Also she works for Mr. January and was probably just helping us to mess with him. Oh, I know! Let's ask your mom, Eleanor. She knows what's going on. She just didn't bother to tell you before she abandoned you and left you to fend for yourself. No one is going to help us. No one. We're on our own."

The last word was strangled, twisting itself into something like a sob or a scream, but Eleanor hardly heard it. She felt cold all over, and she could hear the rushing of her own blood in her ears loud enough to drown out even that incessant ticking.

She wanted to scream.

She wanted to hit something, and she was really afraid that what she wanted to hit was Pip.

"She didn't mean—" Otto started, but Eleanor cut him off, standing.

"My mother wouldn't have left if she had any other choice," she said, and she hated how much every syllable wobbled.

Pip's jaw clenched. "You mean not like mine," Pip spat back. "Except your mom did have a choice, Eleanor. She could have warned you. Maybe then we would have been prepared instead of running for our lives. But she didn't. She just left you. So maybe you're not better than me after all."

Eleanor couldn't breathe. She squeezed her eyes shut so tight little starbursts of color danced behind her lids, and then her eyes snapped open again. She opened her mouth to say something—but she couldn't think of a single thing.

Pip had gone pale. "Sorry. Elle, I shouldn't have—"

But Eleanor whirled and ran. Because if she didn't she was going to cry or she was going to punch Pip in the face and she wouldn't even feel *bad* about it. How could she? How *could* she? She'd thought they were friends, but she'd been wrong. They were just people who spent Halloween together and should have gone their separate ways after. And Otto was probably just too nice to say the same.

She heard Pip call after her, and then Otto say something quietly. She wanted them to chase after her. She wanted them to leave her alone. She wanted . . .

She wanted her mother back. But Pip was right. She'd left, and that was that.

Eleanor had slowed down as she walked around the back of the main school building. She was near the field where she and the others had faced the January Society and tumbled through the door into the gray world. It was just trampled grass now. No sign of any strange door or hooded figures. But the sight still squeezed her chest until she could barely breathe. She leaned against the brick wall behind her and covered her face with both hands. Pathetic. Thinking she could just suddenly have best friends, that they'd care about her even a fraction as much as they cared about each other.

She was alone. She was supposed to be alone, so she was. People always left her. Her mother had left. Her dad hadn't even stayed long enough for her to be born.

"'Kay, could you, like . . . have your panic attack somewhere else?"

Eleanor jerked upright. Mabel and April stood only a few feet away. It was April who had spoken, and April who was looking at Eleanor like she was a weird bug that had wandered into their house.

"April," Mabel said chidingly, but didn't follow it up with anything.

"Private conversation happening here? Hello?" April said, snapping her fingers like she was trying to wake Eleanor out of a trance.

"April, I promise no one would ever care about what you had to say enough to eavesdrop on you," Pip said. Eleanor jerked around as Pip strode up. April's jaw dropped.

"Excuse me?"

"Oh wow, I didn't know human voices could get that high-pitched," Pip said. "Is the screech owl from your mom's side of the family, or your dad's?"

"Whatever, freckles," April spat out.

"Gosh, how am I going to recover from *that* burn?" Pip asked, clutching her hands over her heart.

"Loser," April shot at her, but Pip just snorted.

"Come on, Eleanor," Pip said, and grabbed Eleanor's hand, dragging her off around the side of the building. Mabel gave Eleanor an apologetic grimace as they left.

As soon as they were out of April and Mabel's line of sight, Pip dropped Eleanor's hand like it was a hot plate. Eleanor crossed her arms and didn't look at her. Not yet. She knew her eyes were red and puffy. She hadn't cried, but trying that hard not to cry was almost worse than crying. It left you looking like a wreck.

"I'm really sorry," Pip said dully. "I shouldn't have said that about your mom." It sounded rehearsed. No, it sounded like she was repeating what Otto had told her to say.

"It's okay," Eleanor said, grief twining through her like a strangling vine. They didn't have to be friends. She'd just help fight the curse and stay out of Pip and Otto's way.

Pip stuck her hands in the pockets of her navy blue uniform slacks, her shoulders up and arms stiff. "Cool, then."

"Yeah," Eleanor said. They stood in a moment of awkward, horrible silence. In that silence, Eleanor realized that rain was falling—and shimmering with a faint but unmistakable light.

Someone screamed.

For a split second they looked at each other, unmoving. Then they sprinted toward the sound, back around the side of the building.

Pip was faster, racing ahead, but Eleanor put on a burst of speed and they rounded the corner together.

Mabel stood alone, staring blankly into empty space. She looked at them and blinked. "Have you seen April?" she asked, voice vague and distant.

"What happened?" Pip demanded.

"I have to go find April," Mabel said dreamily. Eleanor's stomach tightened. There was no sign of April—except for a tube of lip gloss, lying on its side in a patch of gray, gooey mud. On the wall above it, the strange symbol from Mr. Maughan's house was gouged into the brick.

Eleanor peered toward the forest on the other side of the field. Something huge and dark lumbered among the trees— and then vanished.

"There," she said, pointing. "Something—"

Pip was already off like a shot. Eleanor ran after, swearing under her breath. Sure. Chase the giant monster. They didn't even have the walking stick anymore!

There were only a few glops of mud to mark the path between the school and the woods. Even the grass stood up straight, hardly bent. If that big thing had passed this way, it hadn't left a trail. But at the edge of the trees were the scattered beads of a bracelet. April's bracelet.

They slowed. Pip's fingers twitched like she was longing for her walking stick, and Eleanor wrapped her hand around the crystal that hung at her neck. "Maybe we should get Otto," she said, but Pip shushed her.

And then, up ahead, she saw it: a shadowy shape, huge and bulky, almost like a bear—but with tattered ears like a bat and a blunt snout. Mud caked its body—layers and layers of mud, dripping down from its thick limbs, running over its face. Pooling on the ground beneath it. April hung limply over its shoulder, eyes shut. Mud covered her face.

The beast started to turn. Pip dodged behind a tree trunk and yanked Eleanor along with her. They crouched, peering out. The creature's head swiveled as it scanned the woods. Through the flowing mud peered two black, lightless eyes. When it peeled its lips back and snarled, its teeth were flat and yellow.

It sniffed the air, making a *slurk* sound like when you have a bad cold and suck in snot. Eleanor pressed herself against the rough bark of the tree, willing it not to see them.

She blinked. It had been there, and then it was gone. She was so startled that for a moment she didn't move, sure that it would reappear. Then Pip waved her forward and they crept toward where it had stood.

They found the mud pit by almost falling into it. It was nestled between tree roots, Mushrooms grew around it in a ragged circle, but they were glowing this time, like they had been when they found the glimmermanders. A viscous bubble rose to the surface of the mud and popped with a wet *glorp*.

"It went in there," Pip said.

"We should—"

"In 'Brackenbeast,' the monster has a passage to his lair. So maybe this is it. That thing took Mr. Maughan through the mud, and now it's taking April."

"Yeah," Eleanor said. "But—"

"You want to just let it take her?" Pip asked, furious. "We have to go in after her."

"But we don't—" Eleanor started. They didn't have weapons, or a plan, or any idea what was on the other side. But Pip only gave a fierce shake of her head—and leaped.

She plunged into the mud and vanished with hardly a ripple. Eleanor sucked in a breath. She stood, hands closing into fists and opening again, for one second, two, three, the ticking of the clock keeping perfect time.

Pip didn't emerge.

Eleanor couldn't let her face whatever was in there alone.

Fine, maybe she wasn't Pip's friend—but Pip was hers. And Pip was right. They couldn't let it just take someone in front of them. Not even someone as excruciatingly boring as April Berry.

Eleanor took off her glasses and zipped them into her rain shell pocket. She took a deep breath. And then she jumped into the mud.

Nine

Eleanor plunged straight down, so fast it seemed like the mud was sucking her in. She had time to shut her eyes tight before it was over her head, and then she couldn't tell if she was sinking or if she was just floating. Was she moving? Or was she stuck?

Ten seconds passed. Then twenty. Her lungs started to burn. Her resolve fractured as fear crept in. She tried to move her arms. The mud dragged at them. She flailed. She was going to drown. She was going to—

Her head broke the surface, and she gasped, getting more than a little mud into her mouth. She couldn't see anything, but when she flailed, her arms hit solid ground. She hauled herself up. She swiped at her face and blinked furiously.

The mud stung her eyes. She fumbled in her pocket for her glasses and put them on, and the trees came into focus. She hadn't just climbed out of the pit she'd gone into. These woods were nothing like the ones she'd left behind.

She got to her feet, turning in a slow circle as she took it in. She stood beside a tall, pale trunk. Into its silvery bark was gouged the same symbol the brackenbeast had left when it took April and Mr. Maughan—except this time, it was pointing upward.

Beyond, the forest spread in all directions, every tree the same silvery pale color. They were spaced far apart, but little grew between them. There was only muddy, trammeled ground, wet from the dripping of water from above. The trees rose up and up and up, with few branches until they reached the canopy. Above, the branches were woven together in a regular pattern, forming a vaulted ceiling, like a cathedral. Only a few shafts of light pierced through, leaving the whole forest in gloomy darkness.

Darkness, except for the glimmering mushrooms that grew among the roots and the mud, and the glimmermanders, here and there, moving among them.

This was not Eden Eld. This wasn't even Oregon. She was in another world.

A shadow moved among the trees. The mud-beast. But where was Pip? She took a step toward it, and something crackled and crunched under her feet. She froze. Then she crouched, feeling in the mud. Her fingers closed around something small and smooth. She drew it out of the mud and suppressed a horrified sound.

It was a small skull with long front teeth. Like a squirrel, maybe, or a rat. And when she reached into the mud again, she felt them: hundreds and hundreds of tiny bones.

She glanced back at the mudhole. The mushrooms around the edges had dimmed, and the last light bled out of them as she watched. She shivered. She had to get moving.

When she walked, the bones crackled under her feet. The sound reverberated through the woods—and yet when the beast had moved away from her, it had made no sound at all. Now she couldn't see it, lost in the gloom, but she moved forward resolutely. Pip was out there. The monster was out there—and it had April. She had to find them.

In no time at all, she was lost.

The trees were arrayed with unnatural regularity, each identical, each placed exactly the same distance from its neighbors. It was impossible to tell where she was going or where she had come from.

"No. No no no," Eleanor muttered. She spun. Where was the mud pit? Where was the way back?

Panic skittered across her back, and she clamped her lips over a whimper. She'd figure this out. She could do this. She started to turn, slowly this time. If she just looked around slowly, looked for footprints or—

A wall of mud stood inches from her nose. A glob of it slid free, falling to the ground with a slap and splash. She looked up. And up. And up. Into yellow teeth, bared in a blunt muzzle. Dark eyes, weirdly dry-looking, ringed with off-white.

The beast growled. She shrieked and scrambled back, hitting the ground. Tiny bones popped under her. She flung herself away from the beast, running as fast as she could as the mud sucked at her feet.

And ran straight into another beast. She skidded to a halt.

But it wasn't another beast. It was the same one. It had the same ears, one tattered, one whole. How had it moved so fast?

She backed away slowly. "Please. Please don't . . ." she said. It dropped down on all fours, advancing with a deliberate prowl. Her mind couldn't quite grapple with how big the thing was. Even on all fours it was as tall as she was, and every one of its limbs was nearly as thick around as her body. Its paws ended in five long claws. Claws just the right size to leave the mark on the back of Mr. Maughan's door. Or tear her into pieces.

It paced around her, sniffing, its eyes fixed on her. She turned with it, her breath hissing between her teeth, her heart galloping wildly. One swipe and it would end her.

An odd hoot echoed from far off among the trees. The beast looked toward the sound, ears sweeping up. It glanced at her one more time—and then it loped off among the trees.

It took her a few seconds to process the fact that she wasn't dead, or about to die. But once she realized it, her legs went out from under her. The relief washing through her was a physical thing, cold and somehow horrible, and she curled in on herself in the mud and tried not to scream.

She did cry. And she told herself *get up get up get up* but she couldn't. Couldn't get up. Couldn't move.

And then she *did* scream. It tore out of her. It was a scream of fear and relief and anger, so much anger, fury at this strange place and at the beasts and at Pip for running off without her and at Otto for not being there, and at her mother and the People Who Look Away and Korri Prosper most of all—

And then there was nothing left to scream at. The forest was silent.

She got to her feet. She was still shaking, but now she felt scraped hollow. And that was better, at least, than being full of all the sharp things that she'd screamed out into the forest.

As the ringing echo of her scream faded, she realized she'd been wrong. The forest wasn't silent. There was still the *drip-drip-drip* of the rain. And the ticking of the clock.

She could hear the clock. That meant this place was connected to her world still. And she could find her way back. Maybe.

"Eleanor!"

Eleanor turned. Pip was running through the trees, mud-covered but alive.

"I tried to follow that thing but it was so fast, and then I couldn't find my way back and I didn't know if you were here and I couldn't find a way out," Pip babbled as she got close. She stopped a few feet away. "Are you okay?"

Eleanor started to answer, but all that came out was a harsh croak. She swiped her hand across her face, trying to get rid of the mud, but only smeared it and made her eyes sting all the more. She turned away, wrapping her arms around her ribs. "I'm fine," she said.

"Right. Just like me," Pip answered softly, and Eleanor let out a strangled laugh.

Pip's footsteps crunched and crackled. Her fingertips brushed the back of Eleanor's elbow, and Eleanor flinched. "Elle. I'm sorry. I really shouldn't have said that stuff about your mom. I didn't mean it. It's just . . . I'm angry all the time, Eleanor. And I know I shouldn't be. And for a while I was doing okay, but when I stop being angry—when I stop being angry, all I have left is being sad and scared. And angry is better. It's easier. It's doing something."

"I know," Eleanor said. She turned. Tears spilled down her muddy cheeks, and she couldn't stop them anymore. "And I know that we're not really friends—I'm nobody, I just happened to be born on the same day, you and Otto don't have to—I'm not—"

"What are you *talking* about?" Pip asked. "Of course we're friends! Elle, you're amazing. You're smart and you're *so* nice and you like listening to Otto, which makes me like you because Otto is the best and if you don't like *him*, I don't like *you*, and you put up with *me* even though I'm a grumpy jerk and I'm ruining *everything.*"

And then Pip was crying. She covered her face and her shoulders quaked and she hunched over as she struggled through the sobs that shook her.

"I'm sorry. I'm so sorry, Eleanor, I don't know what's wrong with me, I just can't stop feeling like this and it's getting worse. I hate her and I want her back and I want her to love me and I want her to be dead. It's too much. I want it to be simple and I want to be over it, but it isn't and I don't know what to do. Just tell me what to do." Her voice broke completely, and all Eleanor could do was wrap her arms around her, all slick with mud, both of them smelling of wet earth and this strange world.

"I don't know how to fix it," Eleanor said, her throat tight with her own sorrow. "I can't change it and make your mom love you. No one can. But *I* love you. Okay? And so does Otto. And so does your dad, and Aunt Josephine. So many people love you."

"I love you, too," Pip whispered.

"Really?" She hated the desperate hope in her voice.

"Really," Pip said. "You're my sister. It just took us a long time to meet so we could figure that out."

"Does that make Otto our brother?" Eleanor asked with a forced chuckle.

"For sure. His mom is going to pass out when she realizes she has another set of triplets," Pip said.

They pulled apart, both of them swiping at their eyes and noses, which only made creative patterns in the mud on their faces. And then Pip burst out laughing.

"You look *terrible*," Pip said.

"Because you look so amazing right now?" Eleanor countered, and they dissolved into giggles. Then Eleanor cleared her throat. "Right. Stuck in a spooky magical forest with monsters. We're never going to find April in all of this."

"We've got to get out and get Otto. We'll figure out a way to help April, but first we have to help ourselves," Pip said. "But I have no idea *how* to get out."

Everything looked the same. So instead of looking, Eleanor shut her eyes. She listened. The drip of water. The soft scrape of salamander bellies in the mud. The clock.

The clock had always seemed to come from all around her, but not here. Here, it had direction. "The clock is coming from that way. Maybe it's coming from our world—and that would mean there's a passage in that direction."

"Decent theory," Pip said. "And better than standing around waiting to turn into more bones for the mud."

Eleanor shuddered. "Yeah. Let's get moving." They started to walk off—but then she grabbed Pip's arm. "Wait. Let's mark the path, so we know which way we came."

She scooped up a big glob of mud and walked to the nearest tree. She dragged the mud across the smooth, pale trunk, writing an *E*.

"It's possible that having a plan is sometimes a good idea," Pip said, giving her a slanted smile.

Eleanor kept her eyes on the trees, fully expecting the beast to reappear—or another one. The one that had examined her was different from the one that had taken April, she was sure of it. Which meant she had no idea how many of those things were in here.

Crunch, crack, crunch went her steps. *Tick, tock, tick* went the clock. Her breath settled into something like a normal rhythm in time to their steps. Nothing lurched out of the dark to snatch them up. Every time they passed a tree, they stopped and marked it with mud, *E*s and *P*s leading in a straight line.

They walked until Eleanor's legs hurt and her body felt heavy, but still the ticking clock came from ahead of her, still nothing pierced the gloom but the shimmering of the glimmermanders.

And then, up ahead, they saw something, a change in the endless rhythm of tree trunks: a circle of dead trees, set closer together than the rest and not nearly as tall, their branches twisting together maybe fifteen feet in the air.

The ticking was coming from that direction.

"Should we get closer?" Pip asked with uncharacteristic caution. Eleanor wasn't sure if it was for her sake or if Pip really was afraid.

"We have to."

They moved forward with renewed caution, but the cluster of trees was completely still. None of the salamanders flickered among the roots, and though the mushrooms grew densely in the mud they were blackened and dull by the time Eleanor and Pip were thirty feet out from the nearest tree.

In the back of her mind, without quite realizing she was doing it, Eleanor counted the trees. Ten, eleven, twelve . . .

"Thirteen," she whispered. Thirteen dead trees in a dark

wood, and the clock ticking loudly in her ears. She gulped. They couldn't run away now. She forced herself forward, balling her hands into fists to keep them from shaking, and Pip walked with her.

The ground between the trees was ridged and whorled, the mud much thicker and formed into a spiral that reached out to each of the trees—or maybe that moved inward from them. Pip stepped onto the thicker mud. It gave beneath her feet with a squish, but there was no crunch of bones, and she stayed on the surface. Eleanor followed. She moved around the side of the nearest trunk—and nearly screamed.

The tree, like all the others in the circle, had a deep hollow at its center, the core rotted out long ago. But the hollow wasn't empty darkness. It had been packed with the thick, stiff mud. And in the mud was a human skeleton.

Its legs were completely buried, but its torso half emerged from the mud, ribs and shoulders and long, white arm bones. Mushrooms, these ones white and twisting, grew through the rib cage and through the eyeholes in the skull. The mud held the head in place, but the jaw had fallen off, and it lay at their feet in another cluster of fungus.

Eleanor suppressed a moan, falling back, away from the tree. But as she turned, she saw that every one of the trees in the circle hid the same horrible secret—the small bones of fingertips poking out of a mass of mud, an empty eye socket peering through the gap in the wood.

Above the hollows, the trunks were marked, again and

again, almost frantic: the downward tree and the upward one, dozens gouged in each dead tree, the smallest the size of her hand and the largest as tall as she was.

The branches tangling above them weren't branches at all. They were roots. The trees had been plunged into the mud upside down, and their roots twisted together not into the woven canopy far above, but into the same shape as the mud. A spiral, stretching inward—but not quite reaching the center.

There was a gap in the roots. A hole in the center and a missing piece of the spiral. It was the same with the mud: a mucky, liquidy splotch in the center, and a section of formless, gooey mud that didn't have the same ridges. Both empty sections led to the same tree. There was no skeleton inside this one.

"Someone got away," Pip said.

"Got away from what, though?" Eleanor asked. Pip only shrugged. Then she pointed.

"There's a footprint."

Sure enough, a single footprint was preserved in the mud where the roots protected it from the constantly dripping water—and it was heading in the same direction as the ticking of the clock.

"Do you think there's someone else here?" Eleanor asked.

"April?" Pip suggested.

"The tracks are too big," Eleanor said, putting her foot next to one of the prints. "And the rest of these people have been dead a long time. Whoever came out of this tree, I think it was a while ago."

"So they're probably dead, too," Pip said. "Or they made it out on their own."

"Or we're wrong, and they need help," Eleanor said.

"Could be," Pip agreed, nodding.

"Right. So." They stared at each other.

"So we'd better follow them," Pip said, not moving.

"Yes. Definitely. We have to." Eleanor took a deep breath. She put her hand out, and Pip grabbed it tight. Together they set out, following the mysterious tracks.

The mud sucked at them, pulling at Eleanor's strength with every step. The cold, dirty water plopped down on her, wetting her clothes, chilling her to the bone. Her breath was ragged, and her feet felt heavier and heavier. Beside her, Pip was struggling, too, but trying not to show it.

"Elle!" Pip said, and pointed. Eleanor's heart stuttered.

Someone was lying at the base of a tree. A man.

"Hello?" she called. He didn't move, or answer. They crept closer. He was slumped down until he was lying almost flat, his shoulders and head propped up. He had long, golden hair, though it was so filthy it was hard to tell. As they got closer she saw that his face had been covered with a giant smear of mud—just like April's had been. He'd sunk down into the mud so far that his lower legs were completely submerged, his feet sticking out. Mushrooms grew all around and over him, sprouting from his clothes, the back of his hand, his cheek, just under one closed eye. Eleanor shuddered. If he'd been lying there long enough for mushrooms to grow on him, he must be dead. And yet . . .

His chest rose and fell slowly. He was alive, but his breath was so shallow and so slow that it reminded her of the hibernating glimmermander.

"Who is he?" Pip asked.

"No idea," Eleanor answered. Something tugged at the back of her mind. Not a memory, exactly, just a faint sense of familiarity that sent an odd, tilting kind of sadness through her.

She knelt beside him and touched a tentative hand to his cheek. His skin was cool. She thought he was about their parents' age—late thirties, maybe. He wore a loose shirt with ties at the neck, and his pants looked like he'd borrowed them from a fantasy TV show.

"It looks like he's reaching for something," Pip said.

She was right: one of his arms was stretched out. A trio of black-capped mushrooms sprouted from the back of his hand where it rested on top of the mud.

In the distance, that hooting sound came again. Another call answered it, and then a third. Eleanor's pulse quickened. She didn't know how she'd gotten lucky, why that thing had left her alone. She wasn't counting on it happening again.

Pip groped around in the mud where the man seemed to be reaching. "Maybe he had something useful," she said. "Could get us out of here. Ugh. This is so gross. And all those bones are poking me. Wait. There!"

She lifted her hand and drew out something long and solid.

A sword.

She had to lift it with both hands to dredge it up, but the mud fell away from it like water, and not a speck clung to the silvery blade. It was three feet long and, from the way Pip's arms strained, very heavy. The hilt was wrapped in soft brown leather, and the mud hadn't stuck to that, either.

Pip glanced between the sword and the man. "No way. You can't be," she told the man.

"What?" Eleanor asked.

"You know," Pip said.

Eleanor looked at her blankly. "I really don't," she said.

"*Jack.*"

Eleanor's eyes widened. "No way," she echoed.

He couldn't be Jack.

That sword couldn't be Gloaming.

Fairy tales weren't real. The monsters were. The wicked men and riddles and traps were real, but the good parts?

The good parts were never real.

Unless just once, just this time, they were. Unless for the first time, someone might actually be able to help them.

Ten

The hooting was getting closer. It was more insistent now, several voices calling back and forth to each other. They had to get out of there. Now.

Jack was the hero in all of those stories. They'd been looking for someone, anyone, who could help them. Here he was. They couldn't leave him behind.

Pip rested the sword against a protruding root so that it wouldn't sink back down into the mud. Eleanor scraped at the mud on the man's face. It felt different from the other mud—stickier, thicker. She had to get her hands wet with the mud on the ground to get it loose, and even then it stuck to his face here and there.

They plucked the mushrooms off his skin and knocked them off his clothes. He didn't stir. "Wake up!" Eleanor told him. She shook his shoulder.

The hooting had gone quiet. Somehow, that didn't reassure

her. They needed to wake him up. But how? "I don't know what to do," she said helplessly.

". . . and sometimes waiting around for a plan just takes too long," Pip said. She pulled her hand back—and slapped the man across the face.

He jerked. Groaned. His head rolled back, and his eyes opened to slits. They were gray, pale, and startling. "Brfnur," he said.

"I don't know what that means. Those big bear-bat-mud things are coming," Pip said.

"'S mucks," he said. Or maybe *smucks*? Eleanor couldn't tell if that was another slurred bit of gibberish or what the things were called, but she'd take it.

"Mucks, then," she said. "They're coming and we can't carry you out on our own."

"And we don't know how to *find* the way out," Pip added.

"So we need you awake. Got it?" Eleanor made her voice as commanding as she could.

"Shtree," the man said. He lifted his hand with great effort, stretching a single finger out. "S'way utt."

Tree. Way out. She looked to the side where he was pointing.

The gouges in the tree had begun to heal over, but they were still visible. A letter carved into the bark. *J*.

"Are you Jack? The real Jack? Are you—" Eleanor started, but his eyes were drooping again. They didn't have time for questions.

He was wearing a sword belt with a scabbard. "Here, help

me get this off. You can use it to carry the sword," she said to Pip. It took some maneuvering to get him rolled over and the belt out from around him, but he offered no objection, only watched them through one half-open eye.

If Pip belted it at her waist it would just drag on the ground, so they looped it over her shoulder instead and put the sword in. "Very cool," Eleanor told her. Pip grinned.

Trying to pull the man up between the two of them was like trying to lift a pallet of bricks. "This just isn't going to work if you don't help," Eleanor told him sternly, knowing full well that it wasn't his fault.

But his lips twisted in what was almost a smile, and the next time they hauled on his arms, he heaved himself upward. It wasn't much, but it was enough that he flopped forward so they could hold his weight on their shoulders. Eleanor braced her feet under her. He shuddered as his muscles strained, and his head lolled against Eleanor's shoulder, but together the three of them staggered forward.

One slow, painful step at a time, they made their way between the trees. She saw the next *J* ahead and angled them toward it. Her legs and back burned. Sometimes his legs gave out, and it was all they could do to keep from dropping him or falling down.

She didn't know how long they'd been walking when he made a noise more like a gurgle than a word and jerked his chin forward.

The mud pit would have been invisible amid all the other

mud except for the perfect circle of glowing mushrooms around its borders. At its edge, a strange construct of branches and twine stood like a signpost: a stick version of the symbol on the trees.

"Almost there," Eleanor told the man.

The flash of movement gave her the only warning before the muck slammed into her.

She went flying. She hit the ground and rolled, and then lay there, the breath knocked out of her. She waited for the crunch of teeth and slice of claws. It didn't come. She rolled onto her belly and pushed herself up on one elbow.

Three of the mucks stood between her and the man, who had fallen in a limp heap. Pip staggered to her feet beside him, moving awkwardly with the sword on her back.

The muck in the center stood on its hind legs, forelegs hanging at its sides like arms. The other two were the ones she'd met already—the one that had sniffed her on the right, the one that had taken April on the left. All three growled at her. The one in the center let out three sharp hoots, then advanced.

Upright, it didn't lumber like a bear—it walked as naturally on two legs as four, hunched slightly forward.

Pip reached up. Her hand closed around the hilt of the sword. Eleanor shook her head. That sword was too big—Pip would barely be able to swing it. And these creatures were huge. "Just go," she mouthed.

Pip drew the sword. As she did, she yelped as if in pain, but then she had the sword out, winking in the light from the canopy. She gripped it in both hands and squared off.

"Back off!" she said, voice shaking. "You don't want to mess with us."

"They're animals," Eleanor called to her, trying to keep her voice quiet, her stance small and unthreatening. "Remember what Otto says. It's about how you sound, not what you say."

"Sound scary. Got it," Pip said. "Leave her alone!" she told them. This time she sounded stern, fierce.

The mucks chuffed and hooted angrily, but they scurried to the side, giving Eleanor a gap, which she dived for, catching Pip's outstretched hand. The man had already started to drag himself across the ground. He was almost to the mud circle.

They sprinted forward. Pip and Eleanor grabbed the back of the man's shirt and hauled with every ounce of strength they had, toppling him headfirst into the mud. He slid in with a slurp.

The mucks howled. Pip and Eleanor held each other's hands tight. They leaped.

The mud took them under.

Eleven

Eleanor and Pip came up spluttering. Even though they'd gone in feetfirst and the man had gone in headfirst, they'd all come up the right way around. The man had managed to grab hold of solid ground, though he didn't have more than his head and shoulders out of the mud. His cheek rested on the ground, his eyes closed.

They weren't in the strange woods anymore. But they weren't in the woods by the Academy, either. Just ahead, the forest gave way to an overgrown orchard, and behind it loomed Ashford House—the house Bartimaeus Ashford had built, and where Eleanor lived now.

Eleanor and Pip pulled themselves out of the mud. Another strange set of sticks and twine was stuck beside this mudhole, but this one was upside down.

Behind them, the mud *blorped*, and a brutish, long-clawed paw thrust up out of it. Eleanor felt frozen in place, but her mind churned. The other holes had closed behind them, so why was this one open? The mucks had carved symbols, and the sticks formed the same symbols—were the sticks keeping the hole open somehow?

"The sticks!" Eleanor said frantically, pointing and hoping that Pip understood.

"Gah!" Pip yelled, and swung the sword. She hacked at the sticks, chips of wood flying. There was a sound like pudding going through a vacuum, and then the paw was gone. The glowing mushrooms went dark. The mud congealed rapidly. "That was close," Eleanor said.

"How'd you know it would shut the mudhole?" Pip asked, sounding impressed.

"Lucky guess," Eleanor said. "They're the same as the symbols the brackenbeasts—mucks?—are leaving, so I thought maybe it was keeping the hole open."

"Nice," Pip said appreciatively.

"If you hadn't leaped into action, it wouldn't have mattered that I figured it out," Eleanor answered.

"Yeah, we're a pretty good team," Pip said.

"Now we've just got to get Otto so he can figure out *why* that worked," Eleanor said, scrunching up her nose. "Because I have no idea."

Pip carefully set the sword down while Eleanor wiped the worst of the mud from her glasses—though this still left them streaky and hard to see through. Then they turned their attention to the man, who Eleanor couldn't help thinking of as Jack.

Getting him out took more effort, and when he was on solid ground he immediately rolled onto his back, eyes shut, and didn't respond to their poking, prodding, or yelling (that last one was Pip). Eleanor vetoed Pip's suggestion of slapping him again, given the lack of immediate danger.

"What now?" Pip asked.

"I'm not sure," Eleanor said. "How long have we been gone? I left my phone in my backpack."

"Me too. I have no idea. An hour? A day? I'm super hungry, and we'd just had lunch."

"Yeah, but you're always super hungry," Eleanor pointed out. Her stomach rumbled. "I'm starving, too."

As soon as they'd been marked absent, the school would've called Jenny and Ben and Pip's dad. Which meant people would be worried about them.

Except that the Wrong Things had a way of folding the world in careful creases, tucking the supernatural parts of it out of sight and out of mind. They might not be looking for her and Pip at all.

Or April, she realized with a jolt of guilt. They'd lost her. She was trapped in there—or dead. It wasn't their fault, she told herself. She'd had no way to find her. They could go back and save April when they understood what they were dealing with.

"What *was* that place?" she asked out loud.

"I don't know. But it reminded me of something," Pip said. "And there's something about that symbol . . ." Her eyes unfocused, but then she made a frustrated noise and shook her head. "I can't remember. I wish I had Otto's memory."

Once Otto learned a fact, it never left his head. Sometimes Eleanor thought his mind must be unbearably noisy, with all those facts and thoughts and ideas zipping back and forth.

"We should probably get moving," she said. "We can go to Ashford House."

"Looking like this?" Pip asked.

Eleanor ran her fingers through her hair and flung a handful of mud to the ground. There were little bones tangled in her hair, too. She scraped all the mud off that she could, as did Pip, but the only thing truly clean at the end of it was the sword.

The sword didn't look quite as intimidating on this side of the mud door. Or, at least, not as long. She'd thought the blade was three feet long, but it was closer to two. And Pip didn't seem to be straining to lift it as much.

"I don't think we're going to get any cleaner," Eleanor said. "Help me move Jack."

When they tried to lift him to drag him along the ground, Eleanor's arms and back protested with a surge of pain, and she dropped him with a yelp.

"I think I pulled something," she complained.

"I can't carry him on my own," Pip replied. "I could—"

"You're not slapping him again," Eleanor said. She considered. "Yet. We'll hold the option in reserve."

"That's all I ask," Pip said generously. To Jack she said, "Hey, you. We'll be back soon. Promise. Don't go anywhere." She tucked the sword and scabbard next to him, patting him awkwardly on the shoulder, and jerked her head in the direction of Ashford House.

They exited the woods and walked through the orchard behind the house. The mud was already drying, turning into a stiff shell that pulled painfully at Eleanor's skin and made her clothes crackle.

They were almost to the house when a school bus pulled up, out at the main road—and a familiar figure stepped off. Otto carried Pip's backpack in front of him, his arms wrapped around it, his own and Eleanor's dangling off his shoulders.

Otto's whoop of joy when he spotted them was the most beautiful sound she'd ever heard. He ran over to them, shouting and babbling so fast she couldn't tell what he was saying.

"You're okay!" Otto exclaimed. "I thought you got taken! Mabel told me you went into the woods and I went too but you weren't there but there was this mud pit like the one we found before but it had dried over and then you weren't in class and no one but me noticed, and I was so freaked out."

"April got grabbed," Pip said. "We went after her. And you're not going to *believe* what we found." She grinned.

"Is April with you?" Otto asked. The smile fell from Pip's face.

"No," Eleanor said. "We couldn't find her. But we saw what took her."

"Mucks," Pip said. "They're called mucks."

"They're like the brackenbeast in the story, but all covered in mud," Eleanor added. They told him about jumping through the portal, and about the strange wood. She told both of them about the muck she'd thought was going to attack her, and then Pip explained about finding Jack.

"Wait. *The* Jack? You're sure?" Otto asked. "What happened to him being an amalgamation? He's *real*?"

Pip shrugged. "We don't actually know if it's him. But he had a sword and he looks like he's visiting from Narnia, so I'd say there's a solid chance."

"Where is he now?" Otto asked.

Eleanor jerked her thumb over her shoulder. "He's unconscious. We don't know what's wrong with him. We need to find a place to hide him."

"The secret room?" Otto suggested. He meant the room hidden behind the fireplace in Eleanor's house—a room that maybe only existed in another world, or maybe in between worlds, but definitely wouldn't be stumbled upon by her aunt and uncle. It was the logical choice.

"If we move fast we can get him in there before Jenny gets back from Naomi's checkup. Jenny told me she'd be gone when I got back from school," Eleanor said.

They tromped back through the orchard, which until today had been the creepiest collection of trees Eleanor had encountered, and back to where they had left Jack. She'd worried they would find him gone—or dead—but he hadn't moved a muscle except for that slow rise and fall of his chest as he breathed. His face was still, but not peaceful, twisted in an expression of distress and maybe anger.

There was something so, so familiar about that face, but she was certain she had never seen this man before.

"Okay. Let's do this," Otto said, rolling up his sleeves dramatically.

"Eleanor and I can take his shoulders, and you take the legs?" Pip suggested. Otto nodded. Eleanor said nothing. "Eleanor?"

Eleanor shook herself. "Sorry. Shoulders. Got it."

"Something wrong?" Pip asked.

"No. Except—does he look familiar to you?" Eleanor asked.

"Not really," Pip said. "But it's hard to tell with all that mud on his face."

"He looks familiar to me. Sort of. I don't know, it's weird," Eleanor said. "Don't worry about it. Let's go."

Pip shrugged. Together, they lifted Jack. If he'd been heavier, Eleanor wasn't sure they'd have made it without dropping him, but whatever had kept him alive hadn't kept him particularly healthy. Now that she wasn't running for her life she could tell he was emaciated, barely skin and bones. Even so, it was a stumbling, awkward trip through the orchard.

As soon as they were inside the door, they had a new obstacle to contend with: Prince Caspian. He came bolting down the hall, having escaped yet again from his room, and skidded to a halt fifteen feet away. His head quirked to the side as he attempted to interpret the scene in front of him—three mud-covered humans and another one, unconscious, being carried between them. He tried growling, then whining, then sitting, his brain not up to the task of deciding on a course of action.

Then, without warning, he launched himself at them.

"Caspian!" Eleanor yelled as he smacked against their shins and snapped at Jack's hair.

Jack thumped to the ground as they lost their grip, almost squashing the little dog. Caspian raced in a circle, barking wildly. Then he dashed off down the hall again and out of sight.

"There is something wrong with that dog," Pip said grumpily as they picked Jack up again. Eleanor just shook her head.

The door to the "secret room" was in the Great Room, the biggest room in all of Ashford House. The walls were lined with bookshelves, and the furniture was the heavy leather sort it would require an entire moving crew to shift. The centerpiece of the room was a fireplace so large you could walk around in it. Weirdly, in the back of the fireplace was a set of stairs leading up and ending in a blank wall of stone bricks.

Or so it appeared. Eleanor reached behind a dusty set of books, all of them ancient. She groped behind *Practical Mycology*, *Legendary Beasts of the Pacific*, and *Cities That Never Were* and extricated the key, which had been disguised as the pendulum of the very clock that ticked away in the background of their existence. The keyhole was hidden behind a false brick. On the other side of the wall was a room that could not possibly exist. There wasn't any space for it in the house—if it really existed, it would have jutted out into the rooms on the other side of the wall.

It wasn't in their world, like the wood wasn't in their world. Otto suspected that it wasn't properly in *any* world, in fact, though his attempts to explain that were a bit circular and rambling. Bartimaeus Ashford had warned them not to spend too much time in it, because it did weird things to you, but they still popped in occasionally to study the artifacts that were stored in the long, museum-like space.

They dumped Jack somewhat unceremoniously on the floor, and then did what they could to make him more comfortable, stuffing Otto's jacket under his head.

"He's not moving much," Eleanor said.

"He's been really out of it, even when he was awake," Pip replied. She knelt down next to Jack as Otto did the same on the other side. Otto checked his pulse and put an ear to his chest to listen.

"His heart is beating really slowly," Otto said.

"The mud was keeping him in some kind of stasis. It must still be affecting him," Pip said.

"How did you wake him up before?" Otto asked. "Maybe we could—"

"I slapped him," Pip said matter-of-factly. Otto blinked rapidly.

"Probably not a solution we can scale up," he said delicately. Pip snorted.

"Those mushrooms were growing on him," Eleanor said. "Maybe they have something to do with it."

"All we need is a degree in mycology," Otto said.

"What did you just say?" Eleanor asked. The word plucked at her memory.

"Mycology. It's the study of mushrooms," Otto said.

"Like *Practical Mycology*? That's one of the books downstairs," Eleanor said, but somehow she didn't think that was what she'd been half remembering.

"Let's go check it out," Otto suggested.

They traipsed down the stairs together. Eleanor found the dusty book right where she'd seen it, on the shelf where they always hid the key. The cover was brown leather, old-fashioned. Its pages were yellowed and its corners were battered. The creases in the binding suggested it had been paged through quite a bit. Some of the pages had come free of the binding entirely and were sticking out a bit from the rest.

The book was mostly taken up with large watercolor-and-ink illustrations, with a brief description on the page opposite, like an encyclopedia of mushrooms. The first entry she flipped to made it clear that the title of the book was misleading. *Practical Mycology* appeared to be anything but practical.

"'*Amanita lacrimae*,'" Eleanor read. "'Or the teardrop toadstool. These minute mushrooms grow only where a lost child's tears have fallen upon the forest floor. Dry, then grind to a powder; mix with mare's milk to invite dreams of places lost or forgotten.'"

The illustration showed a girl kneeling between tree trunks, tears running down her cheeks, as little toadstools grew around her.

Eleanor turned a few pages to pick another random entry. "'*Gomphus labyrinthus*, maze mushroom. Found in certain forests in Wales. When dried and preserved, may be carried as protection against losing one's way. When fresh, may serve as focus to open the way to the endless labyrinth. As no mortal has ever escaped the endless labyrinth, this is not recommended.' Um, yikes."

The picture showed a meaty mushroom, not the type with a cap but more like a lumpy vase. The outside was irregular, but the folds inside formed a minute maze.

Eleanor kept flipping through. There were gravegrabber mushrooms, which grew like grasping hands around gifts left for the dead. Caged ladies, which looked like white nets draped over a disturbingly human-shaped stalk. Mushrooms that smelled like the person you loved and mushrooms that grew out of the skulls of dead bodies and had caps that looked exactly like unblinking eyes.

None of them, as far as Eleanor and the others could tell, were normal mushrooms. And none of them said anything about waking up mud-sick heroes. But still—unless this was some kind of prank book, all of these were supernatural. Wrong Things, or whatever not-quite-Wrong, not-quite-right category the glimmermanders belonged to.

"Do you think these are real?" Otto asked.

"I don't know," Eleanor said. "It's not like *Thirteen Tales*, is it? *Thirteen Tales* is all stories told sideways. Hinting at the truth through fairy tales. This is more straightforward. I thought it would be another book hiding the truth under fiction."

"Fiction . . ." Pip murmured. Then she gasped. "That's what it looked like!"

"Uh. What?" Eleanor asked, looking down at the current page, which showed a mushroom shaped like . . . well, like a butt.

"Sorry. Not that. The trees in the forest. They were woven together like a wicker basket," Pip said. "And it reminded me of something. So did the symbol. I thought I was just re-membering 'Brackenbeast,' but I wasn't. My mom had this book—*Wickerwood*. She read it to me when I was little."

"I have a hard time imagining your mom doing story time," Eleanor said.

"She was really into it," Pip said. And then she paused. "Though come to think of it, she always picked books that scared the pants off me and gave me nightmares. Oh."

"I remember that," Otto said. "That's when you decided you hated reading."

"You're right," Pip said thoughtfully. "I liked it when my dad read the stuff he was translating to me. He always picked the ones I liked. But I thought most books had awful stuff in them, and he was just reading me the few nice ones. So I didn't ever really learn to like to read."

"That's horrible," Eleanor said with feeling. She couldn't imagine having her love of reading taken away from her.

"In the book, there was a witch who had these big bear monsters who kidnapped people," Pip said. "Just like the mucks—except I don't think they were muddy."

"What was she doing with them? The people, I mean?" Eleanor asked.

"A spell, I think," Pip said, face scrunched up as she tried to remember. "She needed a bunch of people for it, but I don't remember what it was for."

"It must be something she can use to capture us," Eleanor said. "Can you remember anything else about it?"

"Not really, but I think we still have it. *Wickerwood*, I mean. But . . . it would be in her office at school. She doesn't keep any of her books at home." Pip swallowed. "We'll worry about it after we wake Jack up." She waved at Eleanor. "Keep going. Please. We're standing here staring at a butt."

They didn't have time to go through every entry in detail. Eleanor started to flip through quickly, fanning the pages.

"Wait, stop!" Otto cried. Eleanor paged back, and there they were: *Rickenella lumen*. The picture was unmistakable, especially as it included a pair of glimmermanders twining among the mushrooms. "'Glowcap is exceedingly rare, growing only in intermundal liminal spaces.' What does *that* mean?"

Pip already had her phone out. "You guys know stuff. Some of us have to learn how to *find out* stuff instead. Voilà." She'd plugged things into a search. "*Liminal* means in-between places. Like doorways, that sort of thing? And *intermundal* doesn't seem to be a word, but *inter* is between in Latin, and *mundus* is, like, world or universe, I think? So that fits. It grows in the spaces between different worlds. Like between here and that weird forest."

"Let's see," Eleanor said, reading the rest of the entry. " 'Characterized by a blue-purple phosphorescent aspect.' Can't this guy just write things normally? They glow! Just say they glow! Ugh. And he doesn't say anything else useful."

Caspian chose that moment to come charging into the room, this time carrying one of Uncle Ben's socks. When he saw Jack in convenient licking range, though, he dropped it and lunged, swiping his tongue over Jack's face. Eleanor grabbed the dog, nearly dropping the book—but then Jack groaned. He rolled his head to the side and cracked his eyes open. "Edge," he said, mumbling.

"What does that mean?" Pip asked. "Edge of what?"

"Edge. W . . ."

"Hedgewitch?" Otto piped up. Jack closed his eyes and nodded, a tiny jerk of his chin. Caspian twisted, launched himself from Eleanor's arms, and snatched the sock back up. He carried it into the corner and proceeded to try to murder it. Eleanor decided not to interfere.

"She's not here, if that's what you mean," Eleanor said. "We've never met her or anything."

"Hrmmgl," Jack said. This was less helpful than perhaps he intended. He coughed, sending out a spray of mud flecks, and tried again. "Was . . . hrbuk."

"This was her book?" Eleanor asked, eyebrows shooting up.

Jack licked his lips. "Hide . . . notes . . ." His eyes fluttered shut, and his breathing changed—he was completely unconscious again.

"Hide notes? What does that mean?" Otto asked, but Eleanor reached up to touch the crystal that hung around her neck. The crystal that revealed hidden things. Maybe . . .

She lifted the chain from around her neck. She put the crystal to her eye as she peered at the book. She gasped—and held the crystal above the page just a couple inches, so they could all see.

The entry for the glowcaps wasn't very long, just a single paragraph. Most of the page was blank—until they looked through the crystal. Handwritten notes appeared.

To Counter the Slumber of Wick

5x glowcap, ok if dark. Fresh preferred. If dry, increased amnt?
1 tsp honey
1 tsp salt (sea salt pref.)
1/4 c olive oil
1 of the glowy salamander things (need name for them. Glowmander? Not enough syllables.)

Mix non-salamander ingredients. Spread paste over sleeper's face. Place salamander on chest. Something happens? Unclear—can't remember.

Eleanor's heart hammered. That handwriting. She knew that handwriting. Knew it by heart, every loop and line.

"Finally, something that reads like it was actually written by a human," Pip said. "For the record, *glimmermanders* is better than *glowmanders.*"

"Agreed," Otto said. "We can get all this stuff really easily. Those mushrooms are still out in the woods, and I can grab Kevin from home."

Eleanor read it again and again, but she wasn't really reading the words. She was just tracing each letter, trying to convince herself that she was wrong. That she wasn't seeing what she thought she was seeing.

"Why *Kevin*?" Pip asked, sounding pained.

"It's a good name! I tried to get my mom to name one of the triplets Kevin, but she wouldn't go for it."

"The triplets are all girls," Pip pointed out.

"Kevin could be a girl's name," Otto replied defensively. "Besides, I didn't *know* they were girls yet. We were still at 'Oh Lord, there's three of them.'"

"Back to the matter at hand . . ." Pip prompted.

"Right. I'll get Kevin. As long as we don't have to hurt him."

"I don't think so," Pip said. "I think it would say."

"Maybe it's some kind of chemical reaction with secretions in its skin? Or something magical. Magical chemistry, is that a thing? I wonder if it's systematic like normal chemistry, or if it's more random. I wish it had more detail. I bet— Eleanor?"

Eleanor suddenly realized she was crying. Fat tears rolled down her cheeks unbidden.

"Eleanor?" Pip asked. "What's wrong?"

"Nothing," Eleanor said swiftly.

"Eleanor. It's us," Pip said. "You don't have to hide things from us."

"I could be wrong," Eleanor said. Her voice was shaky. So was the rest of her. "I just—" Eleanor looked over at Jack. He was asleep . . . probably. But she grabbed Otto's sleeve and motioned at Pip, and led the two of them downstairs, both looking puzzled. In the Great Room she turned to them and took a deep breath. "I think this handwriting . . . is my mom's."

Twelve

"Your mom's? You're sure?" Otto said. "That's wild."

"It's not exactly the same. But the way she writes the *T*s and the *G*s . . . They're definitely hers." It was the same handwriting that had been on the notes her mother left in her lunch box every day at school. The notes that had gotten stranger and stranger at the end, turning into eerie, cryptic warnings. *Beware the gray. Don't trust the backward man.*

She'd been right about everything. Eleanor just hadn't understood.

"You know what this means, don't you?" Pip asked. "Your mom was—is—the hedgewitch! That's why the cat-of-ashes knows her! And Bartimaeus knew your dad. He gave you a message for him. And that makes sense. I mean, if your mom was the . . . hedgewitch . . ." She trailed off, the full implications of this hitting her, and her eyes went wide. "Your mom told you that your dad left before you were born, that he didn't even know about you. And that he was a really good person. But if he was so good, he would have come back."

"So?" Eleanor said—but she knew exactly what Pip was going to say.

"Unless he couldn't," Pip said. "Unless he was, say, under a creepy mud spell in a forest full of bones."

Eleanor swallowed. "In the stories," she said carefully, "Jack and the hedgewitch seemed like they might be a couple. And Jack looks . . ."

"Like you," Otto said. Eleanor nodded. That was what she was seeing in Jack's face. It wasn't familiar because she'd seen him before. It was familiar because she'd seen herself.

She'd imagined meeting her father a thousand different ways, but never like this. Finding her dad had always felt like a fairy tale she'd told herself—and now he was the fairy tale, and she didn't know what she was supposed to be feeling. Joy? Relief?

All she felt was afraid and confused and so, so tired.

"This is so cool," Otto whispered. "Your parents are heroes! Like, actual magical heroes! You're their kid! And you're cursed! That is so . . . cool! My mom is just a librarian! Which is also cool, but not, like, *actually a hero in a fairy tale* cool!"

"This is too much," Eleanor said, shaking her head. The urge to run sent a tremble through her body. She'd wanted this so much for so long. What if he didn't love her? What if he didn't *like* her? What if she was wrong? What if—"I can't do this." Panic put an edge in her voice.

Pip put her arm over Eleanor's shoulders and squeezed. "You don't have to do anything," she said, though her curiosity was obvious. Otto was practically vibrating. Eleanor knew she'd just become a walking manifestation of his favorite fanfiction tropes and, being Otto, he was not going to have an easy time keeping cool about it. She caught Pip giving him a warning look.

"We-don't-need-to-talk-about-it-at-all," he said all in a rush. "It's-fine-it's-totally-fine."

"Okay. So let's . . . let's just focus on waking Jack up," Eleanor said. She was having trouble focusing on her own words. It was all too much to think about. So she just wouldn't. And it wouldn't be true, and she'd go back to not having a dad at all, and if he didn't exist she couldn't disappoint him.

"I'll go get Kevin," Otto said. "Pip, wanna come?"

Pip looked at Eleanor. "You can go," Eleanor said lightly. It wasn't very convincing. She definitely was not looking forward to being alone with Jack-her-maybe-dad.

"I'll stay with Eleanor," Pip said firmly.

"Okay. I'll go in for the extraction solo," Otto said. He rolled his neck. "Wish me luck. If anyone spots me, I'm going to get stuck with the villainous trio."

"Your sisters are adorable," Eleanor told him.

"And sticky," Otto said. "And now they can *talk*. I mean, they could talk before, but now they can *argue*. They can talk you into the ground and they're completely immune to logic. I'm severely outnumbered and you should be more sympathetic.

And I'm being a jerk complaining about my family when both my parents are around and, you know, not evil."

"Yeah, but that was really smooth the way you backtracked," Pip said, rolling her eyes.

"You can borrow my bike," Eleanor told him. Focusing on practical things was easier, but she felt like she was being pulled apart in a taffy machine.

Otto saluted and headed out the back. They heard the back door slam shut—and then the front door opened.

"Hey, Elle. I'm home," Jenny called. Naomi made a happy baby burble. "Where are you?"

Eleanor quickly stuffed *Practical Mycology* into the gap between the cushion and the arm on one of the big armchairs. They'd left the door to the secret room open, but you couldn't see it unless you crouched down—which hopefully Jenny wouldn't. "Back here," Eleanor called. And then she gave Pip a horrified look. "Oh no. Mud!"

Pip looked down at herself as if she had somehow lost track of the fact that she was still covered head to toe in dry gray mud. "Oops," she said, and then Jenny came around the corner.

"What the—" She looked them up and down. Naomi followed suit, gnawing on a chubby fist. Then she shrieked and clapped her hands, clearly amused at Pip and Eleanor's plight. Eleanor couldn't help but smile in the face of her dimpled grin. Sometimes she wondered if it had been worth it, making the deal with Mr. January that put them right back in danger for the chance to defeat him for good. But then she remembered that it was little Naomi who would have been the next child to turn thirteen on Halloween and face the curse, and she knew she would do it all over again. Every time.

Jenny was still clearly waiting for an explanation. "We fell?" Pip offered. It wasn't technically a lie.

"Are you all right?" Jenny asked, concern wrinkling her brow.

"We're fine. Just a mess," Eleanor said. And the dried mud was starting to itch. "Actually, we should probably get cleaned up. I can lend you some clothes, Pip." She was struggling not to sneak a look behind her at the open door.

Caspian's collar jingled. Eleanor looked behind her with a sinking sense of dread. With uncharacteristic poise, Caspian trotted down the fireplace steps, sock dangling from his teeth. He walked straight over to Jenny, plopped down on her feet, and gave a contented sigh.

Jenny frowned. Her eyes got that glazed, unfocused look that people always had around the Wrong Things. "Good dog," she murmured. "Let's go get you some dinner."

Caspian might not reliably know *sit, stay,* or his own name, but he knew *dinner.* As Jenny wandered out, he followed with the discipline of a trained soldier. Eleanor let out a relieved breath and gestured to Pip.

When they got to the bathroom upstairs, Pip turned to Eleanor. "Okay. I just need to say this out loud. We are hiding an unconscious sword-wielding grown man who may or may not be your secret dad in your aunt's house, while your aunt is home, in the middle of the day, so that we can use a glowing lizard to do a magical ritual that we got from your mom, who may or may not be Actually a Witch."

"I should be used to this kind of thing," Eleanor said. "But I feel like I'm going to puke."

"We only actually have, like, seventy-two total hours of direct experience with this stuff," Pip pointed out.

"Which is why we need Jack," Eleanor said. Not "my dad." Jack. She could handle that.

Pip nodded. "He'll be able to tell us what we should do. Or do it for us. Or something. Right? He has to be helpful."

"Pip, neither of us has good luck with adults being helpful. Or parents in general," Eleanor said.

"We're going to figure this out," Pip told Eleanor fiercely, grabbing her shoulders. "And if Jack is your dad? We're going to figure that out, too. If he's awful, we'll—beat him up."

"You're going to beat up Jack. The guy who defeated the Underdragon."

"Meh. Bartimaeus probably made that bit up," Pip said. "Besides, he'll never see it coming. Taken out by a five-foot-tall girl."

"What if he's not awful, though?" Eleanor asked. "What if he's great—and he doesn't want . . . doesn't want . . ." She swallowed. "Me."

"Then he isn't great, he's awful, and we go back to plan A: punching him," Pip said. "And maybe he isn't your dad. The evidence is pretty circumstantial."

"Yeah. Yeah, maybe he doesn't even know my mom. Maybe that wasn't her handwriting. And anyway, what is a hedgewitch? Why would she be the hedgewitch in the stories? They're way older than her. She's thirty-five, not three hundred."

"Yeah. It's probably just our imaginations running wild. And it's a pretty epic origin story, so you know Otto's getting carried away."

"It's all too much. It's just this weight pressing down on me," Eleanor said, her voice distant.

"I know," Pip said.

"Yeah. You do," Eleanor replied. She smiled tightly. "I'm really, really glad I met you, Pip."

"I'm really, really glad you met us, too," Pip said. She paused. "I would hug you, but . . ."

"Right. You use this shower, I'll use Jenny and Ben's. And I'll bring you clothes," Eleanor said with a little laugh.

After she'd dropped off a change of clothes for Pip, Eleanor headed down the stairs and to the *other* set of stairs and back up again to get to Ben and Jenny's bathroom, which was the only other one with both a shower and modern plumbing. Trying any of the others was a proposition more dangerous than diving into a magical mudhole.

Eleanor wasn't sure her clothes would ever be clean again, but she piled them as neatly as she could before stepping into the shower.

Ben and Jenny's bathroom was huge, with a claw-foot tub-shower combo she could have laid down in completely. The water pressure in the old house was pretty terrible, even in the updated sections, and it took a long time to scrub all the mud off her skin. The pipes groaned and rattled the whole time. Ashford House was old and huge, and that made it expensive to maintain. Ben and Jenny didn't have the kind of money to fix it up, and every time Jenny was over at Otto's house she would look at the remodeled kitchen and sigh at the quartz countertops. Once, Eleanor had caught her petting them.

When she was as clean as she could get, she dried off and stepped out of the tub. Her reflection stared back at her from the mirror. With her hair flat against her scalp from the water, she looked like a skinny boy. She wished that didn't bother her. She didn't like being *girly*, exactly. But sometimes she couldn't help wishing she was pretty. Or fierce, like Pip, who seemed to have no idea she was totally gorgeous. Not gorgeous like Mabel, but beautiful in the way a tiger was beautiful—a ferocious kind of beauty.

And then there was Eleanor. Plain brown hair that hung straight to her shoulders. Ears that stuck out a little bit. Face angular in an awkward way, a nose so nondescript it was like someone had just taken the average of all white-girl noses and called it good.

She thought about what Mrs. Prosper had said. Makeup could tell a story by making you look on the outside the way you felt on the inside. But it was the other way around, too. Looking at herself in the mirror made her feel small and awkward and unthreatening.

There were a few SixSeed items from Josephine scattered on

the counter. Eleanor picked one up. Not because she was going to use it. That would have been stupid. Mrs. Prosper was evil, and her makeup probably was, too.

But still. *Enhancement Cream. Unlock the goddess within,* one tube said. *Patented mushroom-based formula revitalizes and nourishes skin to be the best, natural You.*

What if the best "you" still wasn't very good?

"Eleanor?" Pip knocked on the door. "I'm all set, want to head back down?"

Eleanor tossed the tube of cream on the counter guiltily—and then, after a moment's thought, collected all the SixSeed stuff into a bag. She'd throw it out so Jenny wouldn't use it. Just in case.

She dressed quickly. When she opened the door, she did a double take. She hadn't paid attention to what she was grabbing, and Pip was encased in her fluffiest, pinkest sweater. If Pip was a ferocious tiger, now she was a tiger in a tutu.

"For the record, I may murder you for this," Pip said.

"It is *super* comfy, though," Eleanor said.

Pip scrunched the fabric between her hands. "Fine. Yes. It's the coziest, warmest, snuggliest thing I have ever worn and I am still going to murder you."

They had to wait another twenty minutes for Otto to get back, having successfully escaped babysitting duty. He had gotten an actual animal carrier for the glimmermander this time, and they set it down next to Jack while they gathered up the rest of the ingredients.

"Are we sure this is right?" Pip asked, frowning at their little bowl of oily potion-stuff.

"It's right," Otto said. "I checked it three times."

"Then let's do this," Eleanor said.

"Are you ready?" Pip asked.

Eleanor steeled herself and nodded. "Yeah. But don't . . . don't tell him, okay? About me? We have to figure out who he is first. And figure out if we're right."

"Of course," Pip promised.

"You know how I am with spoilers," Otto said, hedging.

"It's not a spoiler, it's a *secret*," Pip reminded him, irritation rough in her tone. "An important one."

"I'm just kidding, Pip," he said. "It was a joke. Of course I'll keep the secret."

"Oh." She rubbed a hand over her eyes. "I'm sorry, Otto. I don't know what's wrong with me these days."

"If we get into *that*, we'll be here all day," he said, and she elbowed him.

Pip held the bowl out toward Eleanor. "Do you want to do it?"

Eleanor shook her head quickly. "No. Nuh-uh. Too weird."

"I've got it," Otto said. "I want to be the one handling the glimmermander, anyway. I think he's getting used to me."

He knelt down and dipped his fingers into the oil. He smeared it over Jack's mud-streaked face, covering him thoroughly from his brow to his jaw. Then he wiped his hand on his jeans—"Otto! I brought a towel for that!" Eleanor exclaimed—and then placed the hibernating glimmermander on Jack's chest.

Then they stood back and waited.

At first, nothing happened. The glimmermander breathed slowly. Jack breathed even more slowly. Neither of them moved.

And then . . .

Nothing happened.

But after that . . .

Still nothing.

"Did we do something wrong?" Otto asked. "Maybe it can't be a hibernating glimmermander. Maybe we got the ingredients wrong? Or your mom did? Maybe—"

Shimmering color wavered over the glimmermander's skin. It uncurled slowly, gave two long, slow blinks, and then marched straight off Jack's chest onto the ground.

The mud flaked away from Jack's clothes, his hair, his skin. The concoction of oil and mushrooms shimmered like the glimmermander's skin and then vanished, leaving his face clean and almost peaceful in his slumber.

And then his eyes snapped open.

Thirteen

A second after his eyes open, Jack gasped. A second after that, he sat bolt upright and launched himself to his feet.

A second after *that*, he fell over.

"Whoa!" Pip yelled. She lunged in to catch him before he could knock himself out again, and between her and Otto they managed to get him leaned up against the display cases that ran down the center of the room. Eleanor hung back, hands twisting together, teeth clamped over her lower lip. "Don't try to get up yet," Pip suggested.

"What are you doing here?" Jack demanded.

Pip and the others looked at each other. "Uh, well. She lives here," Pip said, pointing at Eleanor. "And we're . . . helping?"

"This is Bartimaeus's storeroom, is it not?" Jack asked, peering around.

"Yup. That's right," Pip answered. Eleanor usually took the lead on explaining things, but she was glad Pip had stepped in.

She didn't think she could remember her own name right now. "What about it?"

"It is in Bartimaeus's house. And I know the people who live in Bartimaeus's house," Jack said. "You are not they."

"Forsooth," Pip added under her breath. Jack looked confused. "Who do you know who lives here?"

"The Bartons," Jack said. His voice was baritone and commanding. A proper voice for a hero. "Susan and Dennis Barton and their daughters, Claire and Jennifer. They also have a cat. Her name is Snickerdoodle." Eleanor decided he had to be a hero of legend. No one else could say "Snickerdoodle" with that kind of drama. "Now where is Claire?"

Eleanor felt a jolt of adrenaline. He didn't know. She was going to have to tell him.

"Let us ask the questions for now," Pip said sharply. "What were you doing in that place?"

"The Wickerwood?" Jack asked. "I went to retrieve the blade Gloaming." His brow furrowed. "You were there. You had Gloaming—did you get it out of the wood?"

"It's right here, don't worry," Pip said. She picked it up from where they'd set it on one of the tables and held it out to him. A second after he took it from her, she seemed to realize she probably shouldn't have handed a strange man a sword until they were sure he didn't mean to hurt them, and a worried look flashed over her face.

He half drew it from the scabbard. The scabbard was packed in mud, but the sword was still totally clean. He frowned, drawing it the rest of the way, and then glanced sharply at Pip. "You used it?"

"Not really," Pip said. "I didn't stab anyone or anything like that. I just waved it around and yelled a bit to get the mucks away from you."

"Mucks?" he asked.

"That's what you said they were called. I thought," Eleanor said. "Or, um. I guess you were mumbling a lot."

"I don't know what I was trying to say, but the creatures of the wood are called brackenbeasts," Jack said, eyebrow raised.

"Right. Duh," Eleanor said, her cheeks getting hot. Of course they were brackenbeasts. It was only the name of the whole entire story. Now he was going to think she was a stupid kid. Which she didn't care about. Did she?

"Okay, but bracken is a fern, and there weren't any ferns," Otto said. "Mucks makes more sense. There was *definitely* muck."

"You have a point," Jack conceded. "Very well, mucks it is."

"And the salamanders should be glimmermanders," Otto put in.

"Oh, yes. That's perfect," Jack said approvingly. Then he paused. "I'm sorry, who are you three? How did you find me? What has transpired since I succumbed to the slumber?"

"That's a long story," Pip said. "If you were here when Claire Barton lived here, you've been gone for thirteen years? About?"

"No," Jack said sharply, anger lancing the word. Pip took a step back, startled, as his grip tightened on the sword hilt. "That cannot be so."

"I'm not lying," Pip said. "Right, Elle? Your—Claire moved away from home . . ." *Before you were born*, she didn't say, but Eleanor knew what she meant.

"Almost fourteen years ago now," Eleanor said softly. She stood almost against the wall. She'd folded her hands tightly in front of her. She couldn't look at Jack. She didn't want to look closely enough to see if he really did look like her, or if his eyes were kind or cruel, or if he might, somehow, recognize her, too.

Pip turned a glare on Jack, as if it was his fault Eleanor was in so much distress. Which it kind of was, come to think of it. But Jack's face had gone pale.

"I promised her I would return," Jack said. He sounded lost. "Please tell me you are speaking in jest. Trying to trick me."

"We're not. It's true," Pip said.

"Where is she?" he asked, his voice cracking. "I must go to her." He started to rise, but collapsed again, panting.

"Holy bananas, this is epic," Otto whispered.

The pain in Jack's voice was like a key sliding perfectly into the hole in Eleanor's heart. She knew that pain. Pip opened her mouth to answer, but Eleanor stepped forward. Her voice shook. "My . . . Your . . . Claire is missing," she said. "She wasn't well. Isn't well. She's mentally ill—she was really afraid all the time, of everything. And then when bad things actually came for her . . ." Old grief wrapped its fingers around her throat, strangling her into silence.

"We aren't totally sure what happened," Pip took over. Eleanor's mom had gotten more and more paranoid, between her illness and the fact that evil monsters and a cult were *actually after her daughter.* If she'd had help, maybe it would have turned out differently. Instead, their house had burned down, Eleanor had barely gotten out alive, and her mom had vanished. They'd spotted her once, through the magic window at the back of this very room, but they didn't know where she'd gone from there. "She's gone, that's all we know."

"And who are you?" Jack asked.

"I'm Pip. This is Otto," Pip said. "And this is—"

"Eleanor," Eleanor supplied. "Claire is my . . ." She almost said it. She meant to say it. But the lie emerged instead. "My aunt."

"You're Jenny's daughter?" he asked in surprise. "I didn't realize she had a paramour." He paused. "Ah. You go by Elle, don't you?"

"I used to," Eleanor confirmed. Their names were all palindromes—the same forward and backward. It was one of the ways the people of Eden Eld used to mark the cursed children.

"And would the three of you happen to share a birthday?"

"Yuppers," Pip said.

"And you will be turning thirteen come All Hallow's Eve—this year, if I am not mistaken," Jack said. Then he frowned. "Wait. You said almost fourteen years. That's not—it should be thirteen, if the current cycle has not yet completed."

"We're already thirteen. We ducked the curse. Sort of," Pip said.

He laughed. "Jenny's daughter would be the one to outsmart the old villain. The curse is broken, then? Truly?"

"Ehhhhh," Pip said. She waggled her hand.

"We sort of made a different deal," Otto explained. "We escaped, but then we realized that Naomi, that's Eleanor's . . . sister . . . would just get taken instead in thirteen years, so we got Mr. January to agree to stop trying completely if we could outsmart him and each of his sisters. And one of them's coming after us now, which is how we found you. Because she sent the mucks to steal people and Pip followed one of them and she found you instead."

Jack rubbed his brow. "I apologize. This is a great deal to take in. But I must put aside my wounded heart, for it sounds as if you three are in grave danger—and not you alone."

"Can you help us?" Eleanor asked. She hated how plaintive she sounded.

"I cannot even stand at the moment," Jack said with a hollow chuckle. "But whatever strength and whatever knowledge I have is yours."

"Oh," Eleanor managed. "That's good." And then she burst into tears.

Fourteen

"I'm sorry," Eleanor said, gulping in air as tears and an embarrassing amount of snot streamed down her face. "I don't know what's wrong with me."

"It's quite all right," Jack assured her. Otto put an arm around her, and Pip grabbed her hand. "When you spend all the day wearing armor, standing despite its weight, it is often the moment you remove it that your strength abandons you. For that is the brief moment that you do not need to hold fast to it." His voice was calm and his eyes were sad, and he was so right that she started sobbing even harder.

It took her a long time to stop, but finally the flood of tears dried to a trickle. "I'm okay," she assured everyone at last, disentangling herself. She wasn't okay at all, but she felt like she could get there. She waved Pip and Otto away, wiping at her eyes with the edge of her sleeve. "Let's focus on the important stuff."

Otto and Pip traded off while she collected herself, telling Jack an abbreviated version of everything that had happened since last October. Jack listened thoughtfully, asking questions here and there. Then they'd reached the present moment, and they all fell silent, waiting.

"So?" Pip asked after a few seconds stretched into nearly a minute. "What do we do?"

Jack let out a long breath that was not quite a sigh. "I wish that I could give you a simple set of instructions, but the truth is I don't know very much about the brackenbeasts—mucks. Or the Wickerwood. If I did, perhaps I would have been prepared when I went to claim Gloaming. As it was, I was captured embarrassingly quickly, though I did first find the blade, else I would surely be dead. The mucks placed a foul substance on my face. I lost consciousness, and when I awoke I was in some kind of tree."

"We saw the circle of trees," Pip said. "There were skeletons in them."

Jack grimaced. "They were alive when I was there," he said. "The mucks had gathered around, and a woman was in the center of the circle, chanting. They seemed transfixed and did not notice when I wrenched myself free. I had only the strength to drag myself away—and that thanks to Gloaming. Holding it imbued me with some of its strength, but even that was not enough to reach the exit once more. Slumber claimed me again, and then . . . well, then I saw you, my ladies."

"But you've been to the Wickerwood before," Pip said. "In

the story, right? The one that Bartimaeus put into *Thirteen Tales.* You and the hedgewitch rescued the children of Wick?"

"Ah," Jack said. "How much do you know about me?"

Pip shrugged. "Just what's in the book."

"I haven't read *Thirteen Tales of the Gray* myself, but I have an idea of its contents," Jack said. "The tales within collect altered versions of the acts of my predecessors."

"Predecessors?" Pip echoed.

"It means the people who came before him," Otto said.

"I know, but what does *that* mean?" Pip asked, impatient.

"My name is not Jack," Jack said.

"But you're Jack. You said so," Pip objected, frowning.

"No—I'm *the* Jack. I'm not the first and I shall not be the last." Jack waved at them to sit. "I'm getting a pain in my neck craning to look at you three," he complained. Reluctantly, they settled onto the floor, and he explained. "I do not know the origins of the Jack or his compatriots. Bartimaeus did not, either, only that it is far older than the bargain of Eden Eld and the Curse of Thirteens. In the tales, there are three characters who recur, correct? The hedgewitch, Jack, and the girl with backward hands." At their confirming nods, he continued. "For centuries, these three have always existed: the Prime Stories. But they have not always been the same people.

"They go by different names in different tales. Sometimes Jack is the warrior. The knight. The champion. The hedgewitch becomes the wise woman or the magician or the giver of names. And the girl with backward hands—well. That is the name given to a specific woman who bore, and perhaps still bears, the Prime Story of the wanderer, also called the world walker or the key. Claire Barton is—or, at least, was—chosen by the hedgewitch, though she was only in the earliest stages when I last saw her."

"My aunt was—is—the hedgewitch?" Eleanor asked. Then they'd been right. "What—how did that happen?"

"She helped me," Jack said. "I was injured. Claire found me in the woods and treated my wounds, and that was enough for the story to take notice of her. She took the actions of the hedgewitch, and so its story chose her."

"Then what's your real name?" Pip asked.

Jack gave sad smile. "Jack will do. I've been Jack a long time. And a good thing, too. For there is none better to aid in a fight against dread beasts such as these mucks of yours."

"So you weren't the Jack who fought the brackenbeast," Otto said.

Jack shook his head. "I believe I became Jack sometime in the late 1980s, based on certain, ah, linguistic quirks I still had when I met Claire. Some previous Jack fought the mucks and lost Gloaming. I thought to reclaim the sword, and Bartimaeus told me where it might be found. I thought it would be a simple matter. Clearly I was wrong."

Downstairs, a door slammed, and a voice came floating up, deep and singsong: *"I've got a lovely bunch of takeout food, deedleedeedee here they are a-leaking in my baaaag. Yellow curry, pad thai, some satay on a stick . . ."* Uncle Ben had arrived.

Caspian, overjoyed at the return of his new best friend, lent his howling to the improvised song.

"Who is that?" Jack asked curiously.

"My dad?" Eleanor offered.

"Your parents don't know the truth of this, do they?" Jack asked. Eleanor shook her head. "And it should remain that way. Very well. I cannot stay in this room; I will never heal with its influence around me. Is there a place in the house your parents don't go?"

"Normally I'd say yes, but Ben-uh-Dad is between gigs and he's going through everything to make sure it sparks joy," Eleanor said. Jack obviously didn't understand what this meant, but he nodded gravely.

"Then we will need another safe place for me to recover."

"Mr. Maughan's house," Pip said at once. "It's empty, and the mucks aren't going back there, since he's already gone."

"We'll have to sneak you out," Eleanor said. "It's a long way into town. Can you drive?"

"I can drive," Jack told her, a touch of amusement in his eye. "And I know what television is, and even the internet."

"That does make things easier," Otto said.

Eleanor nodded. "We can use the old car in the shed. It doesn't run very well, but no one will notice for at least a few days if we take it"

"So we get Jack to Mr. Maughan's house. What then?" Pip asked. "What about the people the mucks have taken?"

"You have spoken of two victims. Have there been others?" Jack asked.

"I don't know," Pip said. "Not that we know of."

"Then we need to determine why those two were taken. Then, perhaps, we can discover what this Mrs. Prosper's plan is. And put a stop to it."

"It would help if we knew anything about her," Otto complained.

"But we know lots about her," Pip countered. "We know she calls herself Korri Prosper. And she sells SixSeed. And if Mr. January was like Janus, a Greek god, then maybe she's like a Greek god, too. Goddess, I mean."

"Which one do you think? Aphrodite? That would fit with beauty stuff," Eleanor said.

But Pip shook her head. "Korri Prosper. Korri Prosper. My dad would know this. Prosperprosperprosper—Proserpina!"

"Bless you," Otto said.

"No, Proserpina is the Roman name for Persephone. You know, goddess of the underworld? Wife of Hades? She got kidnapped by Hades and taken into the underworld. She ate six pomegranate seeds, so she had to spend six months out of every year in the underworld. *Six seeds*. And sometimes Persephone is called Kore. Like Korri!"

"So what does that tell us about how to beat her?" Otto asked excitedly.

Pip deflated. "I have no idea," she admitted.

"We'll keep thinking," Eleanor assured her. "We'll figure it out."

"And make a plan?" Pip guessed.

"And get it done," Otto finished.

Together, they could do this. Because, Eleanor thought with both determination and relief, they were friends. "Okay. Step one," Eleanor said. "That book—*Wickerwood*. We should go find it."

"It'd be at the school," Pip said.

"Wouldn't be our first time breaking in," Eleanor pointed out. "We can go tonight, on our way to Mr. Maughan's."

Pip nodded. "As long as I don't have to do it alone."

"Of course not," Eleanor said.

"We'll be with you," Otto promised.

"Not to interrupt," Jack said politely, "but I haven't eaten in over a decade. Could I trouble you for a sandwich?"

The three friends burst into laughter, and Eleanor took off for the kitchen.

Fifteen

Jack could indeed drive—like a grandma. He crept along ten miles under the speed limit and signaled for a full minute before every turn, and Eleanor, sitting in the back seat behind Otto, found herself pushing her foot against the floor as if it were the gas pedal, willing them to go faster. Caspian crouched in her lap—he'd gotten caught chewing on a two-hundred-year-old side table, and Jack would need company anyway.

"Where exactly did you learn to drive?" Otto asked casually.

"Claire taught me. I'm sure I knew at some point before I met her, but I'd been in other worlds a long time by then," Jack said. "It's difficult knowledge to retain, I admit. Driving is not a natural fit for the Jack story."

"Uh-huh. So. Maybe you don't know you can go faster," Otto said.

"This is already unnaturally fast," Jack said through gritted teeth. He had them there.

"Here," Otto said. "Turn left."

They crawled into the turn so slowly Eleanor thought the engine might stall out—but then they were finally pulling up to Pip's house.

Pip stood in the driveway, a black knit cap jammed down over bright hair. Eleanor leaned over and opened the door for her. Jack pulled away and turned around, heading to the Academy.

"Any trouble?" Pip asked.

"No. Ever since Naomi, they go to bed at nine sharp," Eleanor said. "They get up with her a lot in the night, but they never check on me, so we should be safe."

"Your father strikes me as a kind man," Jack said. "I am well pleased that your mother found such a companion." He was right; Ben was the nicest person Eleanor had ever met. He was always making up silly songs for Naomi and kissing her cheeks and making faces at her, and letting her sleep on his big, broad chest for hours at a time.

No matter how great or terrible Jack turned out to be, he couldn't be that kind of dad to Eleanor. It was too late for that.

"How well do you know her?" Pip asked. "I mean, she didn't know about all of this, did she?"

Jack shook his head. "No. But as Claire and I grew close, and began to spend a great deal of time together, it was inevitable that I meet those in her life."

"Jen—my mom never mentioned you," Eleanor said. It was on the long list of things they never talked about.

"I doubt she remembers," Jack said. "She has not the touch of the other worlds. The otherworldly slides away from her memory and her attention."

"We've noticed," Eleanor said dryly. "Did you spend a lot of time here? In our world, I mean? Or are you from a different world, or . . ."

"We Prime Stories tend to roam the worlds quite a bit. Although worlds is perhaps the wrong word for them," Jack said. "This is a world, full and complete. The Wickerwood and the part of the gray you have visited, and others like it—they're more like tidal pools, after the ocean has gone out. Pieces of a world caught behind after the rest has gone. We are most at home in those remnants, visiting your world only when it touches them. But I stayed because of Claire. Most people here thought of me as eccentric, but weren't able to see what I truly was."

Then they'd reached the Academy, and Jack was parking in the back lot.

"Are you coming?" Otto asked. But Jack shook his head.

"I'd best rest," he said. "Besides, someone needs to look after His Highness." He looked pale and exhausted, and none of them objected. Pip let them in with pilfered keys and they made their way through the dark, echoing halls of the school, lighting their path with the bobbing beams of flashlights.

The interim headmaster had been given an empty storage room for an office. Ms. Foster's office remained sacrosanct. No one even went in to clean it.

The interior of the office was all dark wood and leather, with a huge oak desk in the center. They crossed to the bookshelves, splitting up to cover more ground. Most of the books were on education and administration, the sort of thing you'd expect a headmaster to have. There was a shelf of American history and then a small section of books featuring a shirtless, long-haired man apparently named Rafe Slade, with titles like *The Lady and Her Pirate*. Eleanor couldn't decide whether to be amused or horrified by *that* revelation.

"Here they are," Pip said quietly. She was kneeling and looking at the very bottom shelf of a huge bookcase. A small collection of slender volumes was tucked next to a Janus bust, covered in a thick layer of dust. Eleanor's eyes swept over the titles. *The Boy Who Wept. The Game of Bones. Castle of Blood.*

"Those sound cheerful," Otto noted.

"They're horrible," Pip said. Her face scrunched up. "Actually, they're *really* horrible. There's no way I'm remembering these right. They don't put that stuff in kids' books." She pulled *The Game of Bones* off the shelf. It was a slim book, heavily illustrated, and she flipped through to a page near the end. "No. It's exactly how I remember it," she whispered. She handed it to Eleanor.

It was Anna's turn to take the dice. She didn't want to, but her hand closed around them like a claw.

"Throw," said the boy with empty eyes.

"Throw," said the man with no hands.

"Throw," said the woman who wasn't there.

Anna clutched the dice tight. She wouldn't throw them. She wouldn't. But her fear made her shake, and the shaking made her drop the dice. She tried to catch them, but down they tumbled, and struck the ground with a clatter.

The dice were blank. They had always been blank.

"It's not fair. I can't win," Anna cried.

"No, but you can lose," the boy said. He smiled and smiled and smiled.

Eleanor read the rest, even though she felt sick. Things didn't end well for Anna. The illustrations were drawn like they were for a kids' book, with the round faces and bright colors.

The brightest color of all was the red.

She shut the book and put it back. "They're all like that?" she asked. Pip nodded. "Those are not normal kids' books."

Wickerwood, an old, battered paperback with yellowed paper and dented corners, was at the end of the shelf. The cover was white, except for the title and author and a stark black symbol. The upside-down tree and the right-side-up one, side by side so they almost touched.

The author's name was Esther Ashford.

A chill ran down Eleanor's spine. Pip opened the cover and flipped to the copyright page. The book had been published in 1976. The dedication read *To Andy, my favorite nephew, collector of tales and finder of secrets.*

"Andy Ashford," Otto breathed. Like Ashford House. Like the Andy Ashford whose name was inside the cover of *Thirteen Tales*. He'd lived there before Eleanor's family moved in.

Pip's hand hovered over the pages. Then she shut the book. "Let's get Jack to Mr. Maughan's. We can look at it there," she said.

It was sensible enough—but Eleanor wondered, looking at Pip's troubled expression, just how frightening this book was.

JACK NEEDED HELP to get up the steps to the house, and they took him straight to the armchair in the middle of the living room. He sank into it with a groan and closed his eyes. "Sorry," he muttered. "Just need . . . a moment . . ."

His whole body relaxed. He was sleeping, but it seemed like a natural sleep this time, so they padded into the kitchen to let him rest. Caspian trotted after them and scratched at the cupboard until they got him some kibble, then settled under the table.

Pip handed *Wickerwood* off to Eleanor. "Here you go, Miss Speed Reader."

"I read fast, but this is a whole novel, and the equinox is the day after tomorrow," Eleanor said. "You've read it. What's it about?"

"It's been a long time," Pip hedged. But she took a deep breath. "Sorry. It just still freaks me out. It's about two brothers,

Philip and Ivan. They're visiting their aunt, and they find this thicket of brambles in the woods. It's shaped like a tunnel, so they follow it, and end up in the Wickerwood. It's just like the wood that we saw, except without the mud. It's been cursed so that there's no light, and everything in it has died except for these big fat mushrooms and these monsters. They were called . . . I can't remember."

"Fernfolk?" Eleanor said, looking in the book. Pip nodded. "Like bracken!"

"Fernfolk. Right. Only it turned out the fernfolk weren't evil at all, they were under the curse, too. The problem was really a witch. She was forcing the fernfolk to kidnap people for her. She takes Ivan to use him in this ritual. Philip goes to save him. But it doesn't work. The witch drains the life out of Ivan, and then she uses that power to get Philip, too. And it goes into all this detail about the horrible things that she does to them."

But Eleanor shook her head.

"What?" Pip asked.

"That's not what happens at all," Eleanor said. She held the book open to the end. "Look, at the end they're back at home. And it sounds like the fernfolk have been freed from the curse. They're having cake. It has sprinkles."

"*What?*" Pip asked. "Let me see that." She grabbed the book from Eleanor and flipped back and forth. There was Philip defeating the witch. There were the fernfolk, dancing in the sunshine and singing fernfolk songs. "No, this isn't how it ends. The witch wins. The boys die. It's *awful*."

"Your mom read you this book," Otto said carefully. "Is it possible . . ."

"She made up a different ending," Pip said, furious. She flipped back through the book. "This book is completely different than I remember. But look at this." She showed them an illustration—thirteen trees in a circle. They weren't upside down like they'd been in the real Wickerwood, and the people were tied to them instead of stuffed inside, but it was definitely the same ritual. "It says that she's trying to make herself immortal."

"But that's not what Mrs. Prosper is doing," Eleanor said.

"Maybe that part is made up for the book," Pip suggested.

"Children?" Jack called from the front room. Eleanor gave a guilty jump. They'd kind of forgotten about him. They hurried back out to where Jack was waiting, and Otto, being the fastest talker, summarized what they'd found. "The People Who Look Away already possess immortality, or as close to it as they could hope for," Jack said when Otto was done. "That is not their aim. I need to—" Jack started to push himself upright. He got halfway to his feet and then collapsed back into the chair with a rush of breath and a grimace.

"You need to rest," Eleanor said, dismayed.

"What I need to do is help you. You mean to continue your investigation, do you not? Then I will accompany you. Only . . . give me a moment to gather myself," Jack said, but even that effort had left him looking green.

His fall had knocked over the pile of books beside the chair, and they spilled to the ground, the makeshift bookmarks falling out of some of them. Eleanor stooped to pick them up, and her eye snagged on the titles. *Greek Myths. The Mycology Encyclopedia.* She'd seen them before, but she hadn't known what mycology meant until Otto told her, so it hadn't stuck in her mind. Could it be a coincidence? It couldn't be.

"Mr. Maughan was researching the same stuff we are," she said. The book on mycology was about the normal kind of mushrooms, so he couldn't have learned much, but the fact that he'd been researching them at all was weird.

"Do you think he knew something about Mrs. Prosper and the mucks?" Otto asked.

"We never searched the rest of the house," Pip pointed out.

Eleanor glanced at Jack. He had his eyes half-closed. Looking through the house would give him more time to recover. "Let's check it out," she said. "*Then* we'll figure out who's going where, and who's staying in that armchair until they're fully recovered."

Jack gave her a wry smile but didn't protest. Caspian trotted at their heels as they made their way to the back hall. The house was small, and had just two rooms and a bathroom. The first room they checked was a bedroom, and the most unusual thing they found was that Mr. Maughan had over a hundred pairs of novelty socks. The other room was more interesting.

The room had been decked out like a cross between a study and a laboratory. A desk against one wall held books and handwritten notes and a clunky-looking laptop. On the other side of the room was a microscope and chemistry set. The table was absolutely covered with SixSeed products.

"Whoa," Otto said. He drifted over toward the lab equipment. "I think he was analyzing the products."

"Check this out," Pip said, shutting the door behind them and revealing the bulletin board that hung on the wall.

It was covered in printouts and newspaper clippings, all connected with pins and string. There were articles about SixSeed and Eden Eld and the January Society's annual charity auction and about people who had gone missing from the town over the last hundred years. Some of them were crossed out, others circled.

"He's got the Professor Ashford article," Otto noted. It was an article they'd found last year, describing the curse and how thirteen-year-olds kept going missing in Eden Eld.

"He's got us," Pip said.

The photo had been printed out from the computer. The three of them stood together, Pip holding Caspian. Eleanor and Pip were smiling; Otto had gotten distracted by a bird and was looking off the other way. She remembered him snapping the picture. It was the first time they'd met.

"This is creepy," Otto said.

At the center of the board was a photo of a young man, next to another article about a strange disappearance.

Twenty-three-year-old Austin Maughan remains missing three days after his disappear-

ance from his home in Eden Eld, the article read. Maughan's fourteen-year-old brother states that he saw a "mud monster" steal his brother in the middle of the night. His mother, a regional representative for Persephone Cosmetics, claims to have been asleep at the time of the alleged abduction.

"Mr. Maughan's brother was taken by mucks?" Pip said.

"It looks like Persephone Cosmetics is an old version of Six-Seed. They renamed themselves a few years ago," Eleanor said, paging through papers that had been out on the desk. "This says that SixSeed has an office right here in Eden Eld."

"What do you think the SixSeed stuff is for?" Otto asked. "Do the People Who Look Away need money? Do they have employees? Do they pay taxes? How do you get a social security number if you're an immortal being from another world? Do you think they'd get themselves a retirement account to look more legitimate, even though they'd never age enough to have to retire? If there was a company picnic do you think—"

"Otto," Pip said gently. His mouth shut with a click of teeth. "Mr. January used the January Society to do things. Maybe SixSeed is like that. A cult for Mrs. Prosper."

Eleanor snapped her fingers. "The mucks kept sniffing us, but they didn't attack. We must not have smelled right because we didn't have SixSeed stuff on us. They grabbed April because she was using SixSeed stuff—she had their lip gloss, and she said something about her skin, too. And Mr. Maughan must have figured out that SixSeed had something to do with his brother's disappearance, but the mucks followed the scent to him before he could put it all together."

"And then they grabbed him," Pip said. "Game over, Mr. Maughan."

"He's not dead," Eleanor said. "Jack said that when he was in that circle of trees, everyone else was alive. So Mr. Maughan must be, too."

"I get why Mrs. Prosper would want to get rid of someone who knew about what she was doing, but why take April?" Pip said. "I can think of literally zero reasons she would be useful to kidnap."

"Maybe she was just convenient," Eleanor said.

"But Mrs. Prosper doesn't need convenient people. She needs us," Pip objected.

"When Mr. January came after us last year, he couldn't grab us himself," Eleanor said. "He needed the January Society to be the ones that grabbed us to make the deal work. So she's not sending the mucks after us."

"She's going to make us trade," Otto said. "Us for them."

"But that would mean . . ." Pip started.

"Mr. Maughan has been looking for his brother for thirty years," Eleanor said quietly. "When it's family, you don't ever give up. You'd do anything."

"Our families," Otto said, eyes widening. "She's going to go after our families."

"That's why she's giving them all samples," Eleanor said. "I got rid of all the ones that Jenny had."

"I just took the brochure," Otto said.

"But Jojo has tons of that stuff," Pip exclaimed. "We have to get to her!"

Outside, a loud bang echoed through the trees.

Sixteen

The bang reverberated through the air.

"That sound came from your house!" Otto said to Pip, but she was already running. They scrambled into the living room to find Jack trying to push himself to his feet.

"We'll go. You keep resting," Pip said.

"I cannot allow children to face danger on their own," Jack objected.

"No offense, but we've been on our own this whole time," Eleanor said, and she wasn't just talking about last Halloween. "We've managed."

"You should not have to," Jack said simply. Eleanor didn't respond. She didn't know what she could possibly say.

"Here." Pip held out Gloaming. "In case any mucks show up."

Jack put his hand on the sword, but there was an odd hesitation in his movement. Eleanor didn't have time to wonder why. Another *bang!* sounded from the direction of Pip's house. They sprinted out the door and through the trees, Pip in the lead.

Bang!

Bang!

The sounds got louder as they approached, one every minute or so. They skidded into view of the house. Aunt Jojo and Pip's dad were on the back porch, lit by the glow of the porch light. Jojo had her hands on her cheeks in an almost comical expression of shock and dismay, and Pip's dad had his hand on the top of his head, his expression one of confusion and consternation as he spoke into his cell phone.

Bang!

One of the trees at the edge of the backyard cracked. It snapped off about halfway up, a good fifteen feet off the ground. The trunk toppled back, away from the house—and then the bottom half *slorped* down into the ground as if yanked by a giant hand.

Bang! Bang! Two more trees went.

"What's going on?" Pip yelled over the sound.

"I haven't a clue," Jojo yelled back.

"The fire department is on its way. Maybe we should stand clear of the house," Pip's dad said. He blinked at the kids. "Oh, hello, Otto. Eleanor. You're out late for a school night, aren't you?"

"Special project," they chorused.

"Quite a lot of special projects at that school," he muttered, but he was interrupted by another pair of bangs.

And then, suddenly, silence. Whatever had happened seemed to be over.

Sirens blared, coming rapidly closer. Despite the privacy the trees afforded them, it was only a mile to the fire station.

Eleanor and the others were ushered into the front yard, over their strident objections. Josephine and Pip's dad left them, helpless and fuming, to go talk to the firefighters. "Ugh. I wish they'd let us get closer," Pip said.

"You should be glad they didn't freak out that you're carrying a sword around," Otto said.

"I'm not carrying a—" Pip began, but she stopped. Because she was. She held Gloaming by the middle of its scabbard, the belt hanging free. Her cheeks flushed. "I meant to hand it to Jack. I guess I ran out of there without letting go. I was worried about Dad and Jojo."

"It must be like the Wrong Things, because none of the adults have noticed," Eleanor said. "So we're in the clear. And I don't mind having a real weapon around. No offense to the hittin' stick."

"RIP hittin' stick," Pip said mournfully.

Eleanor had *seen* Pip give the sword to Jack. Hadn't she? "Can I hold it for a minute?" Eleanor asked. Reluctantly, Pip held it out. When Eleanor took it by the hilt, Pip didn't let go at first—Eleanor had to tug it out of her grasp. She gasped. "This thing is heavy," she said.

"Not really," Pip said, brow furrowing.

It wasn't hard to hold, but swinging it around would have worn Eleanor out in about two seconds. Holding it felt strange, like her bones were buzzing unpleasantly. It made her want to fling it away from herself. "Here. Take it back," she said. She wasn't sure if she'd learned anything, but she didn't want to hold on to it a second longer than she had to.

As soon as Pip got her hands on the sword, she visibly relaxed. "It is a fine blade, is it not?" she said.

Eleanor snorted. "Right, lady knight. A fine blade indeed," she said. But she eyed Gloaming uneasily. She was *sure* she'd seen Pip give it to Jack.

She had a long time to convince herself otherwise. They didn't get the chance to find out what had happened in the backyard for almost an hour. But finally Aunt Josephine came over to talk to them.

"Sinkholes," she said. "Can you believe it? Sinkholes just opening up in the backyard! They say there's no indication that the ground under the house is unstable, but I will not sleep well tonight, that I can tell you."

"Can we see?" Pip asked.

"It's far too dangerous," Josephine said. "You should just get inside. And shouldn't the rest of you be getting home?"

"Sleepover. Special project," Pip said.

"On a school night? Did Harold okay this?" Josephine asked skeptically, and then laughed. "He's so distracted, there's no better time to get away with a little mischief. Go on, you three. I won't tell."

"Thanks, Aunt Jojo." Pip started toward the front door as Josephine wandered back in the direction of the firefighters.

Upstairs, they turned off the lights in the bedroom so they could see better, and Pip got out her binoculars. She took the first turn examining the backyard, then handed off the binoculars to Otto, and finally Eleanor.

Where the trees had been, there were huge pits of mud, wet and lumpy and gleaming in the lights from the house.

"There are thirteen mud pits," Otto noted, his voice flat.

"It's a threat," Eleanor said. "She knows we're getting close to figuring things out. She's trying to scare us."

"She could send a bunch of mucks through there all at once. Maybe that's what she's planning to do," Pip said. "Maybe they're coming now."

"I don't think so," Otto said slowly. "There aren't any glowing mushrooms, like when the mudholes are active. Besides, the mucks are sneaky when they attack. This was designed to be dramatic and loud, so we'd see. So we'd be afraid."

"Maybe we should be afraid," Eleanor pointed out.

"Oh, we should definitely be afraid," Pip agreed. She stuck her jaw out stubbornly. "But not because she wants us to be."

Eleanor felt a familiar sensation stealing over her. The feeling of a plan starting to form.

"Here's what I think," she said. "First, we've got to make sure the mucks can't get our families. So we have to round up every piece of SixSeed products we can find. We'll bury them in the woods. That should be easy for me, since I just have the samples, and Otto didn't take any in the first place. But Otto, you should still double-check your mom's bathroom. If someone at work gave her a hand cream or something . . ."

"On it," Otto said.

"Jojo takes forever to get to sleep, but then she's out like a log," Pip said. "I can get all her stuff. I'm sure of it."

"Great. Because once we're sure our families are okay, we're going to get Jack strong enough, and we're going to go into the Wickerwood and find the people who have already been taken. We'll wake them up with my mom's ritual, and we'll get out of there." Eleanor wished she sounded confident and authoritative, or at least that she knew what to do with her hands. She settled on crossing her arms and nodding firmly.

"Sounds good," Pip said. It sounded doable. Not easy, of course, but as long as they had Jack with them she believed they could figure it out. "Are you two going to try to get back home tonight?" Pip asked.

"No way I'm leaving you alone in this house," Eleanor said.

Otto nodded. "I'll text my mom and tell her you're having an emotional crisis. She can't get mad at me for helping, especially if Eleanor's here, too."

"And I can just text Jenny tomorrow to say I left early for school," Eleanor added.

"Good," Pip said. She sank onto her bed, elbows on her knees. "That's really good. Because I am really freaked out right now."

Outside, the firefighters were still packing up their truck and her dad and Jojo were still talking, but the house was silent—except for the ticking of the clock.

She's here, the clock warned. *Her day is coming.*

They'd be ready.

Seventeen

They slept for only a couple of hours. Long enough for Pip's dad and Josephine to go to sleep, so that they could sneak out of Pip's room unseen and start collecting everything they could find with the SixSeed logo on it.

They had filled two trash bags with eye shadow palettes, moisturizer, supplements, and even SixSeed brand hair clips (couldn't be too careful) before they slowed down. They checked every drawer, between the couch cushions, the medicine cabinets—the only thing left was Josephine's room. They clustered outside, silent and uncertain.

Pip eased the door open. Josephine slept with her arms outflung, as dramatic in sleep as she was in the daylight. Pip snuck over to her bedside table and plucked a few tubes and pots of various face treatments from it, then stole to the adjoining bathroom. A few minutes later she inched out into the hallway, arms full of booty, and eased the door shut behind her.

Not a peep from Josephine. They all relaxed.

"Pretty sure we got everything. I even went through all her pockets and purses," Pip said.

"I checked her car," Otto added. "There was some moisturizer in the glove box."

"Nice," Pip said appreciatively.

They had three trash bags now, bulging with products and smelling like a botanical apocalypse.

They dragged them out the back door, over to the nearest mud pit. Pip emptied the first bag into it. The boxes and tubes sank slowly but completely out of sight.

They moved on to the next pit for the next bag, and then the third. Finally it was all gone, except for the empty bags. Eleanor smiled in grim satisfaction.

It wasn't victory yet. But it was a good start.

ELEANOR WAS ASLEEP as soon as her head hit the pillow and didn't wake up until Josephine's distressed voice stirred her from her spot on Pip's floor. She yawned as the other two awoke as well.

"I have no idea what could have happened!" Aunt Josephine declared. Pip smirked. *They* were what had happened. Eleanor expected Pip's dad's voice to reply, but the smooth, cool tones that answered Josephine made Eleanor jerk upright and Otto leap to his feet. Mrs. Prosper was here.

Pip bolted for the door, and Eleanor struggled out of her sleeping bag to follow. She and Otto nearly ran into each other at the doorway, but then they were thundering down the steps.

Eleanor skidded into the living room, desperately wishing the pajamas she'd borrowed weren't covered with cartoon cats eating sushi. Josephine was on the couch, her hands over her face. Mrs. Prosper stood calmly before her, the sleek silver suitcase resting beside her. She turned to the three of them, hands folded, and gave that little curl of a smile.

"Good morning," she said. "We're experiencing quite the little mystery."

"What mystery?" Pip asked innocently.

"It's gone. All of it! The samples, the supplies for the party tonight. Everything," Josephine said.

"You mean your SixSeed stuff?" Otto asked, eyes wide, voice a bit squeaky. Eleanor really had to give her friends lying lessons; they were terrible at it.

"Just . . . *poof!*" Josephine declared, throwing out her hands and flopping back on the couch cushions.

"Don't fret. It will turn up," Mrs. Prosper said smoothly. "And don't worry about tonight. I'll provide all the supplies you need."

"Really?" Josephine asked. "But the money—"

"Don't worry about the money. I'm happy to cover the loss for you. I take care of my own," Mrs. Prosper said. She gave the trio an amused look, and Eleanor's heart sank.

All that work was for nothing. And worse, they'd forgotten

about the party. "How many people are going to be coming?" Eleanor asked brightly. She couldn't hide the quaver in her voice.

"Oh, plenty," Mrs. Prosper said, her smile growing wider by degrees. "Your aunt. Otto's mother, of course. And so many, many more. Now. Josephine. Collect yourself. I'll be back to help you get ready. Everything will go off without a hitch."

As she walked past them, she reached out and laid a cold palm against Eleanor's cheek. Eleanor looked up at her, lips parted in surprise and fear—and then rage washed over her. "Why are you doing this?" she asked.

Josephine, still on the couch, didn't seem to hear her. She was chattering away about how kind Mrs. Prosper was, but her voice seemed distant.

Mrs. Prosper's thumb brushed across Eleanor's lips. "You made a deal, Eleanor Barton. A wager with forces far beyond you. You still have the chance to escape your fate. We all get a chance. Even I did. What more do you want?"

"You could do the right thing. You could let us go," Pip said.

Mrs. Prosper's head tilted slightly, an amused expression crossing her face. "Oh, Philippa. Don't look to us for mercy. Even your mother had more kindness in her than me." She patted Eleanor's cheek one more time, and then she drew away. Eleanor shuddered and didn't relax until she heard the door shut.

Tomorrow was the equinox. They were running out of time.

"She's so generous," Aunt Josephine said. "Can you believe

it? But I still don't understand what happened. Someone must have broken in. SixSeed products are valuable . . . but why would they take the ones that were open? They even took the juices out of the fridge!"

"I don't know, Aunt Jojo, but maybe it's a sign," Pip said. "Maybe you shouldn't have the party tonight."

"Don't be silly," Josephine said. "If I don't have the party, how am I going to pay for all the product I lost? Besides, it's going to be so much fun. This might be the kind of thing I can really make work. I need something to work, Pip. I just . . . I need it." She drew in a stuttering breath, and Eleanor realized she was trying not to cry.

Pip sat next to her on the couch and put a tentative hand on hers. "Aunt Jojo? Is everything okay?" she asked.

Josephine blinked away tears and gave a wan smile. "It's fine, Pippi. Nothing to worry about. Just grown-up stuff."

"I'm thirteen. I'm not a kid anymore," Pip reminded her.

"Thirteen," Jojo said with a sigh. "I remember thirteen. Thirteen is when I decided that boys might have a use after all." She winked. Eleanor noticed that Pip and Otto got very stiff with the effort of not looking at each other.

"Boys are just as useful as girls," Pip said. "Gender doesn't have anything to do with it."

"Oh, that's not what I meant," Josephine said with a wave of her hand.

"Please don't have the party tonight," Pip said. "I can't tell you why. But you can't do it. Please."

"It's really that important to you?" Josephine asked. She looked puzzled and concerned.

"It is," Pip confirmed.

"Then I'll cancel," Aunt Jojo said.

Pip grinned with relief. "Thank you, Aunt Jojo," she said.

"You're welcome. And now you get off to school. You don't want to be late."

Pip, still grinning, led the way back upstairs.

The sword was out on Pip's bed. She frowned at it. "Did one of you put that there?" she asked.

"No," Eleanor said.

"Wasn't me," Otto said.

"Huh. Creepy," Pip replied. "We'd better get it back to Jack. I can't believe I ran off with it in the first place."

"We'll be late for first period," Eleanor fretted.

"No one shall be much shocked at my absence," Pip said.

Eleanor blinked at her. "What now?"

"No one's going to be surprised I'm late," Pip said, as if she were repeating herself exactly and Eleanor was the one being weird. "And you could use a little more rule-breaking in your life."

"All right," Eleanor conceded, but her stomach churned with anxiety. She hated being late to things.

At Mr. Maughan's house, Jack opened the door at their first knock. He looked better, and not just because he was upright. He had more color in his cheeks, and though he was still thin, he didn't look *quite* so skeletal. He'd also brushed his long blond hair and changed into some of Mr. Maughan's clothes, including an argyle sweater vest that weirdly worked for him.

"I brought your sword back," Pip said. She held it out, but Jack didn't reach for it.

"Why don't you come in," he said. He stepped aside, and they walked past him.

"So do you want this?" Pip asked, holding out Gloaming again.

"You can put it over there on the table," he said, gesturing toward the kitchen. She shrugged and did as he said, though at the last minute she seemed reluctant to let go, and shivered when she did. "What happened last night?"

They relayed the events of the previous night, and he listened with his usual serious consideration.

"It sounds as though you've stymied Mrs. Prosper's plans regarding Josephine, at least for the time being," he said when they were finished. "Well done."

"Thanks," Pip said.

"We really should get to school," Eleanor said, glancing fretfully at the clock on the microwave.

"Yeah. We'll check back right after," Pip said.

They started to leave. Then Jack said, "Eleanor, could you stay a moment? I'd like a word."

Eleanor froze. Pip and Otto were clearly ready to jump to her aid, but she waved them off. "I'll catch up," she promised, and turned to face Jack.

Neither of them said anything until the front door shut.

"We need to talk," Jack said.

"Do we?" Eleanor asked.

"I spent the evening in your house. I heard Jennifer and her husband talking. I know that you are not their daughter. I want to know why you lied to me."

Eleanor gave a strangled kind of laugh. "Isn't it obvious?"

"Are you Claire's daughter?" Jack asked flatly.

She didn't answer. But he nodded. She cursed herself—she should have lied. But what could she say?

"And your father?" he asked. The look in his eyes—was he hoping for her answer, or fearing it?

"She never told me his name," Eleanor said.

"Ah," he said. He wandered over to the chair and sat down in it heavily. "Fourteen years."

"You were trapped. It's not your fault," Eleanor said. "Except, my mom seemed to think you'd meant to leave for good. Did you?"

"It is a complex matter," Jack said.

"Kind of seems yes-or-no to me," Eleanor retorted. "Why would you leave her?" *Why would you leave me?* she wanted to demand, but he hadn't known about her. It wasn't fair to blame him for that.

Her heart didn't care about fair.

"I did not tell you the whole truth about the Prime Stories," Jack said. "Jack, the hedgewitch, the world walker—they are stories. Compared to people, they're simple. People are made up of many stories—the stories they tell about themselves. The stories other people tell about them. The stories around them that they only touch on tiny parts of. But Jack and the world walker and the hedgewitch, they're singular. One story, clear and simple. It makes them strong. But it makes them inhuman."

"You're saying you're not human?"

"The person I once was is gone. I don't even remember him. I don't remember his name or his parents or where he was born. Or when, for that matter. I've been Jack too long to be anyone else." He gazed out the window, into the darkness of the trees. "There used to be so much more of me that wasn't *him*. But that's why I left Claire. The man I was, the man she loved, had faded so much that neither of us could see him any longer—or even know who he had been. We only knew he was gone."

"And what about her? Is that why she left me? Because she was turning into the hedgewitch?" It would explain it, at least. It didn't make it easier, but a reason was more than she'd had in all this time.

"I don't know. But it seems plausible. If she lost too much of herself, she might not know to come back—or it might not be safe. The hedgewitch is more complicated than Jack. Jack is loyalty and protection. The hedgewitch seeks knowledge—the knowledge of how to defeat her enemies. She always works for the greater good, but sometimes that comes at the expense of those around her. With the three of you being so precious to the People Who Look Away, it's possible that Claire didn't feel the hedgewitch could be trusted around you."

"You're talking like they're separate people."

"It starts that way. And then you simply become the Story," Jack said. "It's a curse, Eleanor. As surely as you are cursed, so am I. And so is your mother."

"I'm sorry," Eleanor managed.

Jack stood. "I cannot be a father to you," he said. Eleanor sucked in a sharp little breath, dizziness sweeping over her. "I wish I could," he added. "But Jack is not a father, and efforts to defy him have only ever led to . . . well. The story attempts to correct itself."

That sounded ominous. "I understand," Eleanor said hollowly. Of course she understood. He didn't want her. He was Jack, and Jack didn't have a child, and so she was nothing to him.

"Good. I'm glad," he said. He gave a sharp nod. "It's good to have all of that out in the open."

"Right," Eleanor said dully. "Yes. I should . . . I should go." She straightened up her spine. Squared her shoulders. She turned, and walked out, and she didn't cry.

This didn't change anything. She didn't have a father yesterday. She didn't have a father today.

Nothing at all had changed, she told herself, and knew it was a lie.

Eighteen

Pip and Otto were waiting for her down the path. When they asked if she wanted to talk, she could only shake her head. She knew she should explain about the Prime Stories and the curse, but it was too much right now. They walked to school together, and with each step it got more and more impossible to say anything.

The three of them conferred in hushed whispers throughout the day, whenever they could snatch a few seconds together. Unfortunately, their teachers had caught on by now that when they were sitting together they paid less attention to their work, so they had to restrict their discussions to passing periods and lunch.

They all agreed that going back to Mr. Maughan's—and to see Jack—was the logical next step. They needed to coordinate with him, whatever they were doing next. But Eleanor wasn't exactly looking forward to seeing him again.

It had started to rain once more—as if they needed more mud in their lives. With their hoods pulled up and their shoulders hunched over, they ran for the relative shelter of the trees. Only when they were on the footpath to Mr. Maughan's house did they slow down, panting.

"You'd think after everything we've been through, rain wouldn't bother us," Otto said.

"I love the rain," Eleanor said. "I love it hitting the window while I'm inside with a fire, a cup of cocoa, and a good book."

"Don't forget the fuzzy sweater," Pip said.

"The fuzzy sweater goes without saying," Eleanor replied.

"Guys," Otto said, low and urgent. He pointed out between the trees.

A dark mound of shadow lurked not far away. In the gloom of the woods, it was hard to make out. It could have been a fallen log—until it started to move. It came forward on all fours, a rolling gait that covered the distance impossibly fast even though it hardly seemed to be moving. When it was twenty feet away from them, it stopped.

It was a muck. One of the ones that had attacked her in the Wickerwood, she thought—the smaller one, with the tattered ear. "Stay back," Pip warned.

It charged.

Someone screamed. It might have been Eleanor. All three of them ran, bolting down the path as the muck chased them, its feet making not so much as a whisper on the ground. And then it was on the path in front of them, ears pinned back, eyes fixed on them. They skidded to a halt. Pip shoved her way in front, holding—holding Jack's sword.

When had she gotten Gloaming?

"You can't hurt us," she said. "It isn't the equinox. You can't—"

The beast charged again, and this time there was no time to run. There was only the suddenness of it, the bulk, the sheer mud-coated mass hurtling straight at Pip so fast she couldn't react—

Something dark and fluffy dropped out of a tree and straight onto the muck's head. The muck let out a howl and veered off the path, swatting at its head as its attacker clawed and hissed and spat, sparks arcing from between her teeth. "Go on, kids! I'll catch up with you up ahead!"

It was the cat-of-ashes. "What are you doing here?" Eleanor demanded, stepping forward.

The muck stopped bucking long enough for the cat-of-ashes to fix Eleanor with a split-second glare. "What about this says 'stop and argue,' you whiskerless fool?" she asked. "Go!"

They ran again. Every so often they heard a hoot or a howl from the muck or a yowl from the cat-of-ashes, but there was something strange about the sounds—there was no crashing. Even flailing and fighting, the muck's heavy body and thick limbs made no noise at all.

They reached Mr. Maughan's house and Otto hammered on the door. As soon as it opened they piled in, each of them babbling an explanation. Apparently they didn't do a great job, because Jack finally threw up both hands.

"One at a time, please," he pleaded, and pointed at Otto. Wrong choice.

"We-were-walking-here-from-school-and—"

Jack held up his hand again. "Mercy, Otto. Have mercy."

Otto took a deep breath and tried again. "We were on our way here and a muck attacked us."

"And I have your sword, I'm sorry," Pip said, and she shoved it into Jack's hands.

"I thought they couldn't come after us directly," Eleanor said.

"That was just a guess," Pip pointed out. "We don't know how these things work."

"But you got away," Jack observed. "Did it follow you?"

"The cat-of-ashes saved us. She attacked it," Eleanor said.

"Who is this, then?" Jack asked.

"She's a friend," Eleanor said.

"No, she's not," Pip countered. "She works for Mr. January."

"Not because she wants to. She's a captive," Eleanor said.

"We don't know what she is," Otto said, splitting the difference before they could start bickering. "But she helped us more than she hurt us last time, so if she's here it's probably a good thing."

"You're sweet to say so, child," the cat-of-ashes said, sashaying in through the still-open front door.

Caspian, who until this moment had been enjoying a piece of jerky under the table, shot toward her, barking. Everyone jumped—except the cat-of-ashes, who raised one big paw, flexed her sharp, hot-as-coals claws, and yawned.

Caspian stopped dead. Her mouth shut with a click of teeth, and she blinked lazily at him. "Still want to try it?" she asked.

Caspian trotted delicately back beneath the table. The cat-of-ashes chuckled and leaped up onto the TV stand, settling onto a copy of *Scientific American* and wrapping her tail around her feet.

"Where were we?" she asked.

"Wondering what you're doing here," Pip said, crossing her arms.

"Checking on you, of course. My master wants to know how his sister is doing, and he sent me to collect information. He forgot to tell me to do it without being noticed, though, so . . . here I am." Being a cat, she didn't shrug, but you could hear it in her voice.

"We're doing fine," Pip said.

"But we could always use more help," Eleanor added.

"Oh, I can't help you," the cat-of-ashes said, all wide eyes and innocence. "That would be against the *rules*."

"Are you . . . are you going to help Mrs. Prosper?" Eleanor asked, a little wounded.

"That would also be against the rules," the cat-of-ashes said smugly. "Besides, I don't like her. She's a dog person. You should *see* the beast she has back home—but we're getting off topic."

Jack stepped forward. "If you will not aid these children, and you mean to lend no aid to their enemy either, why reveal yourself? And does attacking the beast not break your rules?"

The cat-of-ashes blinked at him. "Hello. Who's this fellow, then?"

"This is Jack," Pip said. "The Jack. From the stories."

The cat looked him up and down. "Oh, *that* Jack. Frankly, I don't see the appeal."

"She knows my mom," Eleanor told Jack.

"Claire? Do you know where she is?" Jack asked, voice hoarse with hope. Otto looked like he was going to swoon.

Eleanor wondered what it would feel like to be like Claire and Jack—real, sweep-you-off-your-feet love. Or Ben and Jenny, who adored each other so much it was funny. Or even Mr. and Mrs. Ellis, who loved each other with a kind of contentment that you could feel radiating off of them when their eyes met across the room—a split second of serenity even with the triplets and Mr. Ellis's menagerie of half-rehabilitated animals running around. ("I wanted two kids! One dog! Quiet Saturday mornings!" Mrs. Ellis was known to declare at random moments.)

The story of Jack apparently had room for that kind of love. Just not for her.

"I don't know where she is at the moment," the cat-of-ashes said. "But I saw her not six weeks ago, pinkling. She's still alive. Not quite herself these days, though."

"What does that mean?" Eleanor asked. "What happened to her? You told me she didn't set that fire."

"No, I asked who told *you* she set the fire," the cat pointed out. "I made no claims to the contrary." Her ear twitched. "But, oh, fine, I'll be straightforward for once. Tiresome as it is. No, she didn't. The January Society started worrying she'd actually manage to keep you out of Eden Eld long enough to foil them, and they went after you. She held them off. I'm not entirely sure how the fire got started, but she was protecting you."

"Then why didn't she come back?" Eleanor demanded. "Where did she go?"

"She wasn't in a fit state to protect you," the cat said. "More than that, I can't say."

"Why not? Mr. January won't let you?" Eleanor asked bitterly.

"Claire asked me not to," the cat-of-ashes said. They stared at her. She yawned. "She made me promise. And I can't break promises, so you're out of luck. Sorry."

"Let us turn to the task at hand then," Jack said, though from the strain in his voice he wanted nothing more than to interrogate the cat and learn everything she knew about Claire.

"Like I said, can't help you much. But Miss Priss was trying to cheat, so I'm just balancing the books."

"Cheat?" Otto echoed. "How was she cheating?"

"Tick tock says the clock, and it isn't her day just yet," the cat-of-ashes replied. "She put her mark on you and sent her beasts to catch you. We're allowed to stalk and follow before the given day, not snatch you away." Her tail thrashed. It might have been anger at Mrs. Prosper, but Eleanor couldn't help but wonder if it was frustration at not being allowed to go after them.

"What mark?" Eleanor asked.

"Check under your collar," the cat said, purring.

Eleanor craned her neck but couldn't see. Pip peered at the skin beneath her collar, then gave a little exclamation. "There's dried mud at the base of your neck," she said.

Eleanor swiped at it. Reddish-gray, claylike mud came away on her fingers. Not quite the color of the stuff in the Wickerwood, and it had an odd, metallic odor to it. How long had it been there? Mrs. Prosper must have put it there when she touched Eleanor's cheek.

"I'd better clean this off," Eleanor said.

"Scrub well," the cat instructed her. Eleanor hurried to the bathroom and scoured her neck, twisting to see the spot in the mirror. In the other room, she could hear the others' voices as they talked to the cat-of-ashes.

She walked back in, and Pip looked at her. A cold jolt of shock went down Eleanor's spine. Pip's hair was loose and wispy around her face. Dark circles shadowed her eyes. It was just her . . . but there was something off.

Her eyes, Eleanor realized. The color of her eyes was wrong. Muted, somehow.

She must be imagining it.

The cat-of-ashes stretched and then plopped to the ground in that cattish way that made her seem both elegant and like she weighed eight times more than she should.

"I'm afraid I must be going," she said. The tip of her tail twitched like a little wave. "If you run into any more trouble, give me a yell. I won't answer, of course, but yell away." She winked. Then she fixed her eyes on Jack. "And listen, tomcat. You do right by your kit. Got it?"

"My breath, my blood, my bone to keep her safe," he said, and the pledge seemed to make the air hum.

The cat snorted. "We'll see. And I'll see all of you again soon—one way or another."

"Wait," Eleanor said. "Is there really nothing else you can tell us?"

The cat-of-ashes seemed to give this genuine thought. "My master's day runs from midnight to midnight. The one you call Mrs. Prosper keeps different hours. Sunset is your warning this time. When the sun goes down tonight, you're in trouble. And that really is all I can tell you. No, wait. One more word of advice." She leveled a disgusted look at Caspian. "Lose the dog."

With that, she trotted out into the woods and vanished.

"Don't listen to her, Cas," Pip told Caspian. He crept out cautiously, sniffing to make sure the bad cat was gone, and Pip scratched him under his collar.

"It's almost sunset *now*," Otto said uneasily. "I thought we'd have hours left."

Pip's phone buzzed. She stopped scratching Caspian to pull it out of her pocket. "My dad just texted," she said. " 'Staying at Eleanor's tonight? House is beset by womenfolk.' Beset by . . ." Pip frowned and punched in a reply. When the next message arrived, she gasped. "Josephine's party. It's back on. They're there now!"

"Mrs. Prosper must have talked her out of canceling. We have to get over there!" Eleanor exclaimed.

"Then let us make haste," Jack said, which was definitely the coolest way to say "let's hurry." He buckled the sword belt tightly over his hips and then, with a sharp intake of breath, he unsheathed Gloaming. He stood a moment, hand gripped tight over the hilt, then nodded once.

They piled out of the house, Caspian at their heels.

Nineteen

The windows glowed between the trees, a cheerful golden light to lead them on. Eleanor could hear the thump of her pulse in her ears. Cars cluttered the driveway. How many victims did Mrs. Prosper have in there?

"Pip, wait. We need a—" Eleanor began.

"No time for plans!" She sprinted for the front door—and the shadows sprang forward to meet her.

Two mucks reared up in front of her, baring their fangs in silent fury. Pip skidded to a halt. "You can't hurt us!" she said. "It's not the equinox yet! The sun's still up!"

"No, but they can stop us from getting in there," Eleanor said.

Jack stepped forward, drawing Gloaming. His hands wrapped tight around the hilt, his knuckles white. "I'll hold them back," he said. "You three go."

The mucks spread out to bar their way, but Jack darted in,

lunging with Gloaming and forcing them to part. "Now!" he cried, and the three teens darted forward through the gap he had created. As Pip raced past him, he swung Gloaming again, and the sword sang through the air. Caspian lent a ferocious barking to the effort, startling one of the mucks into rearing back.

Eleanor, Pip, and Otto burst in through the front door and thundered into the living room. "Stop!" Pip yelled. The babble of conversation lurched to a halt. There were Jenny and Otto's mom and Susannah Chen and June Berry and other women Eleanor knew from town, standing in a rough circle. Boxes disgorged tissue paper in shades of white and purple. Gift bags were scattered over every available surface. The air was thick with the perfume of a hundred different scents, all of them intoxicating.

At the far end of the circle, Josephine stood, a smile fixed on her face—and Mrs. Prosper's hand on her shoulder. Her fingers were curled under, tight enough to dimple the fabric of Josephine's shawl.

Otto's mother was holding a pot of something that looked like cream and smelled like cinnamon. Pip lunged, smacking it out of her hand. "Don't touch that stuff. It's dangerous!" she yelled.

Otto's mother snatched her hand back in surprise. "What on earth are you talking about, Pip?" she asked.

"Pardon Pip. She's not feeling well," Josephine said. Pip whipped her head in Josephine's direction, and when she spoke again, Eleanor could see that Mrs. Prosper's lips moved slightly, as if speaking the same words at exactly the same time.

"I feel *fine*," Pip said.

"What exactly is going on here, Josephine?" Susannah asked.

"I think we should ask Pip that," Otto's mother said. "What's dangerous, honey?"

Eleanor stared into Mrs. Ellis's concerned eyes. She was a children's librarian—gentle concern was an artform to her. She kept her hair in locs that she swept up in a knot at the back of her head. She'd known Pip since the day she was born. If anyone would believe them, it was her.

And then she looked at Jenny, who had dressed up a bit for what was her first outing in weeks—it must have been a relief, to get some adult interaction after being with Naomi all day. Eleanor moved to stand by her side. If anything went wrong, she had to protect Jenny. She couldn't let Naomi lose a mom, too.

Jenny put a hand on her shoulder, her face a picture of worry.

The others, though—the others looked confused. Hostile, even. June's face had the pinched look of quiet, suburban mom rage. Eleanor wondered if she had even noticed her daughter hadn't come home, if some corner of her mind was frantic with worry—or if the magic of the Wrong Things kept her from feeling anything about it at all.

Josephine was smiling. Smiling and blank-eyed, with Mrs. Prosper's fingers dug tight into her shoulder. A tiny, dark stain spread from the point where Mrs. Prosper's fingernail pressed—a drop of blood.

"I—I—" Pip said. Her eyes were fixed on that small, spreading stain.

"The makeup is dangerous," Otto cut in. "There was an article online."

"I'm afraid you're misinformed," Mrs. Prosper said, her voice like honey. "All of our ingredients are perfectly safe and perfectly natural. It says so in the brochure."

As one, the women in the circle unfolded the brochures they had in their hands and looked down at them. Identical smiles spread across their faces—except for Jenny and Mrs. Ellis, who looked up at Pip again. *Listen to us*, Eleanor willed them.

"Better to be careful, don't you think?" Eleanor said. She took Jenny's hand and squeezed, hoping to pull her attention away from Mrs. Prosper and her strange control. "You're still breastfeeding. You have to be extra cautious."

"Jenny, I'm not feeling too well," Mrs. Ellis said pointedly, giving Jenny a meaningful look as she stepped forward and took Otto's hand. "I'd better head out, and since I'm your ride . . ."

"Right," Jenny said, nodding.

"I'm sure we have something that can fix you right up," Josephine said. Her eyes were blank, like two shiny pebbles. "Stay. Have a few morsels."

Jenny's hand started to slip from Eleanor's grip, but Eleanor held firm. "Let's go," Pip said.

The three of them, along with Jenny and Mrs. Ellis, started to move toward the door. Every one of the other women watched them go with sharp, hungry looks. Their hands gripped the brochures they held so hard the paper crinkled and crumpled. Jenny and Mrs. Ellis looked uneasy.

"Stay," Josephine said.

"Stay," murmured the other women.

"You have a home when you have SixSeed," Josephine intoned.

"Let's *go*," Otto said, yanking on his mom's arm, and then they were hurrying out the door—Jenny and Pip first, then Otto and his mother, and then Eleanor—

The door slammed shut in front of her. She yelped and stumbled back as a gray, mud-caked body dropped from the high ceiling of the foyer, where it had been clinging, flaring its tattered ears toward her.

"It's rude to leave a party without saying goodbye to your host," Mrs. Prosper said.

Eleanor turned slowly.

Mrs. Prosper slinked closer. "I love this part," she confessed. She sighed and ran her fingers over her perfectly coiffed hair, her eyes closed momentarily in sublime pleasure. "It's so, so much better when they know what's coming for them. And so let me tell you what's coming for you, Eleanor Barton. The loss of everyone you hold dear. And then I will have won, and proved my brother a fool."

"Such a fool," murmured her chorus behind her.

"Let them go," Eleanor said, trying to sound brave.

"No," Mrs. Prosper said simply. "I'll keep them, thank you. And Philippa's father, too."

"Where's—"

Mrs. Prosper pulled something out of her pocket. Mr. Foster's phone. Mrs. Prosper waggled it. "He's resting. He has been for hours now," she purred. Which meant he couldn't have sent the text. Mrs. Prosper had sent the text to get them there, all because she wanted them to see how hopeless it was.

Eleanor wanted to find the perfect words to fling at Mrs. Prosper to make her quail. To make her feel small, the way Eleanor felt. The words wouldn't come. But that was all right. This wasn't the time for speeches. It was time for action.

Eleanor lunged past Mrs. Prosper, toward the collection of juice cleanses and perfumes gathered at the center of the coffee table, a collection of jewel tone bottles. She grabbed the edge of the table and heaved as hard as she could, flinging the flimsy table to the side.

The bottles went flying, and the air filled with the sound of shattering glass. A rank, fruit-soaked smell filled the air, and the women seemed momentarily shaken from the spell Mrs. Prosper had them under. They yelped and scrambled, tripped and stumbled, and Eleanor charged through them. If she could get to the back door—

Something huge smacked into her. Warm limbs thick as tree trunks wrapped around her, and together she and the muck hurtled through the air. Over the back of the couch. Through the plate-glass window at the back of the house.

They hit the ground and rolled, Eleanor's vision reduced to a wheeling slice of grass-sky-grass-house-grass as the muck's body cushioned her fall. The muck's grip loosened, and she squirmed free, smacking against the ground belly-first and then scuttling back on all fours.

The muck reared up. It lifted one massive paw, its claws sharp and glinting.

It froze. Mrs. Prosper stood at the broken window, her lips bent in that unworried smile. She gave Eleanor a little wave.

The muck dropped back to all fours and shuffled away, huffing. Otto and Pip chose that moment to come running, but Eleanor waved them back. She stood, panting for breath. Mrs. Prosper and her new servants made no move to stop her.

Eleanor limped over to Pip and Otto. "Let's get out of here," she said. "It's too late for them."

"My dad—" Pip said.

"She has him. We'll get him back," Eleanor said fiercely. Pale, Pip nodded. "Where's Jack?"

"He's gone," Pip said. "He wasn't out front. Neither were the mucks."

They came around the side of the house to see Jenny and Mrs. Ellis waiting anxiously near the back of the line of parked cars, next to Mrs. Ellis's massive van.

Everyone piled in, and Mrs. Ellis pulled away. She eyed the three of them in the rearview mirror.

"Any of you want to explain what that was all about?" she asked.

"Chemicals!" Otto said. "And also their stance on racial justice is wishy-washy."

"Don't just say 'chemicals.' Everything is chemicals. What you have a problem with is synthetic chemicals without adequate trials to establish their safety and efficacy," Mrs. Ellis lectured.

"Yeah, that," Otto said, still a bit out of breath. He sagged against his seat. "Could we talk about it later?"

She pursed her lips but said nothing more. Jenny's fingers worried at the sleeve of her cardigan, tugging at the threads. She had the weird, twitchy energy people got when they strayed a little too close to noticing the Wrong Things and couldn't handle it. Getting a little twitchy was the mild version. Pip and Otto had told Eleanor about people having seizures or hurting themselves if they tried to understand the Wrong Things and their brains couldn't handle it. Eleanor opened her mouth to say something distracting to get Jenny to stop thinking about it, but then Mrs. Ellis uttered a string of words Eleanor had never heard come out of her mouth and slammed on the brakes.

They all jerked forward against their seatbelts as Jack, mud-streaked and with five bloody stripes down his chest, staggered in front of the car, holding Caspian under one arm.

Pip and Eleanor, in the middle row, were the first out of the car as Mrs. Ellis hollered at them to stay put. Otto was only a couple seconds behind as he scrambled from the back row.

"Are you okay?" Eleanor asked. At least Jack was upright.

He winced but nodded. "My injuries are superficial," he

reassured them, handing a thrashing Caspian off to Otto. "And one of the benefits of my affliction is rapid healing."

"Kids, get back," Mrs. Ellis said. Both of the adults had gotten out of the car, Mrs. Ellis with her keys sticking out between her fingers like brass knuckles. But Jenny's mouth was open in a little O, and when Jack saw her he straightened.

"Jennifer," he said warmly. "It's been too long."

"*Jack*?" she said, incredulous. "What are you—in the forest— what the—" She looked from him to Eleanor. "Hold on. You know each other?"

"We, um. Just met," Eleanor managed.

"Do you know—" Jenny stopped. Looked at Jack. "Do *you* know—?"

"I promise, if I had known, things would have been different."

"You broke her heart," Jenny said accusingly. "You just vanished."

"It was beyond my power to return," Jack replied. "But that does not absolve me. I should never have left."

"Wait, *you* knew?" Eleanor asked Jenny.

"Hold on," Mrs. Ellis cut in, holding up a hand. "I'm sorry. Could I get a little bit of context here?"

"Jack's Eleanor's dad," Otto said. He seemed taken aback by his own conciseness, but then nodded in self-satisfaction.

"Good lord," Mrs. Ellis said. She rubbed her forehead. "This sounds like a conversation you should all have indoors. And are you bleeding?"

"No," Jack said firmly. Mrs. Ellis's eyes got a bit distant. Jenny frowned. Neither of them objected to this obvious lie.

"Get in," Mrs. Ellis said with a sigh. "I'll drop you all off."

WHEN THEY PULLED up in front of the house, all of them got out. "You're staying here tonight?" Mrs. Ellis asked Otto.

"Yeah," he said. "We have—"

"A special project," Mrs. Ellis said. She frowned and looked at the house, and then off into the distance. "I want to keep all my babies safe. But you won't be safer at home tonight, will you?"

Otto swallowed. "No."

"I can't keep my mind fixed on what's happening," she said. "It's like . . ." She shook her head. "You'll be home soon," she finished firmly. "You will do what you have to do, and then you will come *home*."

"I promise," Otto said.

"Good." There were tears in her eyes and a shiver in her voice, but then she took a deep breath—and they could see the knowledge falling away from her. Her face grew calmer, her shoulders relaxed. She smiled. "You kids have fun. I'm going to go barricade myself in my brand-new bathroom and take a long soak in my brand-new tub, and nobody's going to try to sell me anything. I think my evening has improved."

She waved a cheery farewell to Jenny and slid back behind

the wheel. As she pulled away, music started blasting from the minivan speakers.

The gray world and the Wrong Things tried to make you be alone. They took away the people who might help you—who would give anything to help you.

The only people the Wrong Things couldn't take away were Pip and Otto.

"Coming in?" Jenny asked. Her cheer was more delicate than Mrs. Ellis's, with Jack still standing right in front of her. "Do you want some coffee, Jack?"

"I would greatly appreciate such hospitality," Jack said. "And to meet your husband, about whom I have heard wonderful things."

"Right. This should be interesting," Jenny said distantly, and led the way up the long pathway to the front door. "Ben should be putting Naomi down for bed soon—"

As she said this, the sounds of Ben's off-key singing came down the hall. "*Everybody is kung-poo fighting! These toots are fast as lightning,*" he warbled, followed by Naomi's pleased giggle. He swooped into view, Naomi in his arms, and stopped dead.

They all stared. He was wearing a fluffy white bathrobe that came down to his knees, showing off his impressively hairy legs. He'd recently shaved off his lumberjack beard, the better to plant raspberries on Naomi's irresistible tummy, and his face was caked with a red-gray mud mask.

Eleanor's stomach dropped.

Caspian yipped happily to see his friend and trotted over to sniff Ben's ankles. Ben grinned at them. "Whoops! Wasn't expecting company," he said. Caspian woofed in welcome.

"Clearly," Jenny said with a little laugh.

"Is that SixSeed?" Eleanor asked, fear in her voice.

"Uh, yeah. I stole it outta that goody bag Jenny brought home. Why?" Ben asked.

"Wash it off," Eleanor said urgently.

He chuckled. "Do I look that scary?"

"I'm serious. You have to get that off right now," Eleanor said. "It's—it's really dangerous—there are these chemicals—" Her mind went blank, dread seizing her.

Naomi gabbled a laugh and reached for her mother. Pip let out a shriek of alarm. Mud dotted Naomi's nose and smudged her round cheek, and her dark baby curls had a streak of mud dried into them.

"Get a washcloth!" Otto yelled. Pip raced for the bathroom down the hall as Jenny and Ben looked at them in bewilderment.

"I feel fine. Maybe a bit itchy," Ben said.

"They're up in arms about it, I don't really understand it," Jenny said. Pip sprinted back toward the entryway, washcloth outstretched. Behind her, the front door was still open. And outside, the sun was beginning to set.

"Close the door!" Eleanor called. Jack stepped up and shut it, throwing the locks. His hand was on Gloaming's hilt.

"I don't understand what's happening," Ben said.

Jenny took Naomi from him, fear beginning to match her confusion. She drew close to Ben.

"Please," Eleanor said. "Get it off. Quickly."

Caspian had gone quiet. He stood facing the hallway, his hackles raised and a growl rumbling in his throat.

"They're already here," Jack warned. He stepped forward, drawing his sword.

There were four of them this time. One in the drawing room, ghosting over the sill of an open window. One clinging to the ceiling of the hall. Two on the double staircase leading up to the second floor.

"Get the mud off of her!" Eleanor screamed, and Pip reached for Naomi.

The muck in the drawing room charged. The one in the hallway scuttled along the ceiling, and the ones on the stairs leaped from above. Pip touched the washcloth to Naomi's face—and then a muck tossed Pip aside. She hit the ground on her side as Jack rushed in, swinging Gloaming.

"Great Room!" Eleanor yelled. The secret room. Maybe it would be safe.

The mucks shrank back from Gloaming, but Jack's arms shook. Eleanor and the others backed away as a group, collecting Pip as they went.

"What are those things?" Jenny asked in a whisper, clutching Naomi against her.

"Bad news," Otto answered.

The mucks shifted, like a ripple going through them. They were getting ready to charge. "When we get to the hall, run. Run for the fireplace," Eleanor instructed.

The mucks charged. Jack lifted Gloaming—but then he cried out and almost dropped it. "No!" he yelled. "She's just a child!"

He swung the blade wildly. It slashed across a muck's arm. Milky white liquid that stank of rot gushed out of the cut, and the muck roared in pain. It slapped at Jack with its other paw.

Gloaming flew from Jack's hand. It slid across the floor.

Pip stuck out a foot and stopped its momentum. And then, without hesitation, she lifted it.

The air seemed to change. The *world* seemed to change. The mucks moved slowly, like they were trapped in molasses. Pip seemed brighter. She leaped forward, and it was like she was flying. The sword moved with her, the sword *was* her, and as its point carved a line across the shoulder of the biggest muck she cried out in triumph. She spun, catching the next muck's swipe on the flat of the blade. It should have wrenched the sword right out of her hand, but instead she twisted, slicing the muck's paw. It reared back with a horrid hooting and she followed up with a thrust at its shaggy torso. The sword squished, past the mud, past the thick fur, and sank into skin. That rotten smell and milky fluid gushed out.

"Pip!" Eleanor yelled. They needed to retreat. But it was like Pip didn't hear her at all. She lunged forward and grabbed Pip's shoulder. Pip whirled, blade raised, teeth bared. Eleanor stumbled back.

Pip sucked in a breath. Her eyes focused. "Eleanor?"

"We need to go," Eleanor said. She held out her hand. Behind her, Naomi wailed in terror.

Pip grabbed her hand. They ran. Otto was already in the fireplace, fumbling with the lock.

They hadn't seen the fifth muck, clinging silently to the ceiling above Ben and Jenny. "Look out!" Pip yelled.

It dropped. With one swipe of its paw, it scooped the wriggling, thrashing baby from her mother's arms. Jenny screamed. Ben roared and he threw himself at the massive beast.

There were two reasons it worked, Eleanor realized later. The first was the creature's surprise at Ben's absolute ferocity, as evidenced by the befuddled look on its ursine face.

The second was that Ben wasn't trying to fight the muck. He wasn't trying to protect himself, either.

His shoulder struck the muck's chest, his body already turning so that he could grab hold of Naomi, lifting her from the muck's bent paw. He kept turning. He threw her, and his momentum carried him back, off his feet, into the embrace of the muck as it wrapped its limbs around him.

Jenny screamed again. Jack lunged, catching Naomi in mid-air, and dropped to one knee so he could scrub her cheek.

The floorboards buckled under the muck and Ben. Ben thrashed in its grip, eyes wide with fear—but then his eyes fell on Naomi, safe in Jack's arms as Jenny raced toward her.

In the instant before he vanished into the mud, the muck dragging him under, Ben smiled.

"It's open," Otto hollered.

Jack grabbed Jenny's arm, holding Naomi fast in the crook of his elbow, and dragged her up the stairs as she called Ben's name. Pip stood at the mouth of the fireplace, Gloaming brandished before her. Hot tears ran down Eleanor's cheeks. Ben was gone.

The four remaining mucks stood in a semicircle below. They swayed, a low moan sounding from all four throats in unison.

Pip and Eleanor turned and ran, Caspian at their heels, as the sun slipped below the horizon and the clock chimed its mournful warning.

Twenty

The door slammed behind them. One of the mucks thudded against the other side, then scrabbled at the lock, but Eleanor wasn't worried about them breaking in. Bartimaeus had made this place as a sanctuary. He'd built it strong enough to withstand a few monsters.

But the damage was already done.

Jenny took Naomi back from Jack, quieting her cries with soft shushes even as she struggled to hold back sobs. She sank to the ground clutching her daughter, and Eleanor knelt beside her, arms wrapped around her. Prince Caspian crawled over and curled tightly against Jenny's side, as if he could sense they shared a great loss.

"He's not dead," Eleanor said. "We can get him back."

"How do you know that?" Jenny asked. Naomi quieted, nestling against Jenny's shoulder with a few little hiccups of distress. "What were those things? What is *happening*?"

"You don't want to know," Pip said.

"Those things took my husband. They tried to take my baby. And Jack is here out of nowhere after fourteen *years* away?" Her jaw clenched. A tendon trembled in her neck and her limbs quivered, but Eleanor could see her fighting the forgetting. "Tell me. Please."

"We call them mucks," Eleanor said. "They're taking people for Mrs. Prosper."

"Why?" Jenny asked. "What does she want with Ben?"

"She doesn't want Ben, she wants us," Eleanor said. Jenny pulled away to look at her. "I can explain, but it might be dangerous."

"Tell me," Jenny said through gritted teeth.

"I can try," Eleanor said cautiously.

"Try what?" Jenny asked, face going slack. Eleanor's breath hissed out between her teeth.

It was no use.

"Pip," Jack said. His voice was grave.

Pip looked down at her hand, still holding Gloaming. "Oh, right. Sorry. Your sword." She held it out—but Jack didn't reach for it.

"It isn't mine," he said.

"I thought it was Jack's sword," she said, puzzled.

"Gloaming is Jack's sword, but I'm afraid that I am no longer Jack."

"What does that mean?" Pip asked.

"I believe it started when you found me in the Wickerwood, and wielded Gloaming to protect me. You saved me, driving off the beasts. Just as Jack would do," he said. Eleanor's stomach twisted. *No.* "Every step of the way you have charged into danger to protect others. Jack was already done with me, I think. I failed in the Wickerwood. The story needed a hero, and I didn't fit the role any longer. But you did. That is why you couldn't give me Gloaming in the house—and you didn't even realize it. It's why I cannot wield it any longer. You are becoming Jack—and I am ceasing to be."

"You can stop being Jack?" Eleanor asked.

"Usually, the story only ends in death," Jack said. "But sometimes the Story chooses to move on. It's not something you can predict or control. They are capricious things."

"You mean . . . I'm a hero?" Pip asked. Her voice was fizzy with excitement. A magic sword, a destiny—it was like every one of her favorite stories. The joy on her face was electric—and Eleanor choked back a sob. "Is that why I could fight so well? Am I going to get other abilities?"

Jack looked at Eleanor. "You didn't tell them?"

"Tell us what?" Pip asked.

Eleanor's hands shook. She balled them into fists. "Being Jack isn't a good thing," she said. "It's a curse."

"But I'm not *actually* Jack. I'm me," Pip said.

"For now," Jack said. "But the Prime Story will write itself over your soul."

Eleanor watched as Pip's fizzing excitement curdled into dread. "You're saying that Jack will . . . what, take over me?"

Jack nodded. "At first you won't notice it. But the more you act in the ways that Jack acts, leaping into danger, defending the innocent, facing down monsters, the stronger he will become, and the quicker your beautiful, complicated self will be erased." He knelt. His hands covered hers, resting on Gloaming's hilt. "Jack is a curse, Pip. They all are. Sooner or later, Jack will take over completely. You'll be him. Or her, rather. The Stories are adaptable that way."

"Then what happens to you?" Pip asked.

"That I don't know," Jack said.

Pip stared down at the sword, turning it this way and that. She didn't look afraid. She looked almost content. "You know," she said softly, "I don't feel sad anymore. Or angry."

"Sadness doesn't suit the Warrior," Jack said, and maybe the sorrow in his voice was proof that the story was leaving him.

Eleanor's stomach was one big knot of dread and horror. She'd just met Pip. They'd just gotten to be friends—she'd just realized how much they mattered to each other, and now she was fading. How long would it take? How long before Pip stopped being Pip at all?

She met Otto's eyes. He looked as afraid as she felt. But Pip was smiling a soft, fierce smile.

Jack took the sword belt from around his hips and wrapped it twice around Pip's waist, buckling it into place. It fit her perfectly. "I wish very much that I could have known the woman you were meant to become," he said solemnly.

But he wouldn't. Because she would never be that person. She would never grow up, not really, never fall in love, never get a job, graduate from college. Jack might do some of those things, but it wouldn't be *her*. Pip would be gone.

It was too terrible to think about. Too immense and frightening in a way that not even the People Who Look Away frightened her.

"Can I do anything for you?" Jack asked.

Pip shook her head. "I guess not. Unless you have any how-to-be-Jack tips." She sounded so, so brave. So much like Pip. Maybe Jack was wrong. Maybe she was too strong for the story.

"You don't need any. It will come to you. And you would do best to resist," Jack said seriously. "Claire stayed herself for many years even after I left, by the sound of it. You might do the same."

"Don't be Jack. That means don't protect people. Don't go fighting monsters and saving the innocent."

"That's right."

But Eleanor knew immediately that it wouldn't work at all—and sure enough, Pip shook her head. "Then it's not an option. We made the deal with Mr. January to protect Naomi and the other kids after us. I can't stop now just because I've got *two* curses."

"It's no wonder the Jack chose you," he said sadly.

Eleanor wanted to say something that would make it better, that would make it not true. She opened her mouth, searching for the perfect words—

And behind her came a sharp, precise rapping.

Someone was knocking on the window.

Twenty-One

Eleanor turned warily. The magic window in the back of the room, which looked out on strange landscapes that shifted constantly, now showed the Wickerwood: the silvered trunk and woven canopy of branches, the darkness and the fragmented lights of mushrooms and of salamanders. Mrs. Prosper stood in her pencil skirt and blazer, standing atop the mud and not sinking into it a centimeter. She gave them a wave with the tips of her fingers and then folded her hands.

Caspian growled and rose, standing between Jenny and the window with his teeth bared.

"I thought this place was hidden," Eleanor said uneasily.

"From my brother, maybe," Mrs. Prosper said. Her voice was clear, only the slightest bit of distortion caused by the glass between them. "But I'm the one who gave Bartimaeus this marvelous glass. I may not be able to reach you in that room, but I can see you just fine. Now, come closer. We need to have a conversation."

Otto, Eleanor, and Pip glanced at each other, gathering strength and confidence for a moment before they walked forward, Jack beside them. Caspian whined worriedly. Mrs. Prosper had eyes only for the three of them, and her smile had a hungry edge as they drew close. She laid her fingers against the glass, almost a caress, and gave a little sigh.

"Ah, I can feel you even through the watching window. So close to sunset, and you're thrumming with potential. What a marvelous key you will make."

"Fat chance," Pip snapped.

"My brother is fond of chance. He likes a touch of the unpredictable. I prefer order. Balance. Day and night, life and death. For every gift a sacrifice. And so I am going to give you a choice. I have your uncle, Ms. Barton. And your father and aunt, Ms. Foster. And little April and her mother, and so many more. You wouldn't believe how easy it is to get people to accept a free gift. They'd feel *bad* for turning it down."

"Great. You're evil. We get it," Pip said. "Can you get to the part where you offer to let them go if we turn ourselves over?"

Mrs. Prosper's mouth got small and pinched-looking, irritation creasing her brow. "Why would you—"

Otto sighed. "You just said you don't like taking chances. You want to skip past the whole maybe-we-win, maybe-we-lose part by making a deal."

"You three think you're very clever, don't you?" Mrs. Prosper asked. It didn't sound like a compliment.

"I mean, we're not stupid?" Pip said. "And it kinda seems like you think we are. And one of the things about low expectations is they're really easy to exceed."

"Well. Yes. Fine. If you turn yourselves over, I'll . . . let the captives free," Mrs. Prosper said with a flourish of her hands. It seemed like the finish to a nice dramatic speech she'd been planning. Eleanor smirked.

"Nah," Eleanor said. "We're good."

"But—"

"'Kay, we're going to figure out how to beat you now," Pip said. "Bye!"

"You—"

"Byyyeeeeee," Otto said, and leaned forward and pulled the curtains shut over the window. The sound of Mrs. Prosper's voice cut off abruptly. Caspian's warbling growl turned into a squeak, and he trotted forward with his head tilted, as if confused about where the mean lady had gone.

"You didn't even consider accepting the bargain?" Jack asked.

Pip shook her head. "No way. Whatever they want us for, it's not going to be good for the world anyway."

"That was actually kind of fun. Did you see her face?" Eleanor asked.

"She looked like—" Otto pulled up his lip and widened one eye in a cartoonish expression of disgust and rage. "Worth it."

"Totally worth it," Pip agreed.

"But we still do need to figure out how to save everybody and beat Mrs. Prosper," Otto pointed out. "I guess you do have a magic sword now."

"Yeah, but in *Wickerwood* the witch can't be hurt with weapons," Pip said.

"That is so," Jack said. "The People Who Look Away cannot be harmed by even a blade like Gloaming."

"How do they beat the witch in the book?" Pip asked. "The real book, I mean, not the way that my mom told it?"

"The brothers trap her in another world, one she can't escape," Eleanor said. "But I don't know how we could do that."

"I still don't understand what Mrs. Prosper is doing with the trees," Pip said. "I get taking our families, but she kidnapped Mr. Maughan's brother decades ago. And Jack here got grabbed before we were even born."

"There's one place we might be able to find more information," Otto said. "The SixSeed office. It's right in town."

"You really think Mrs. Prosper keeps anything there?" Eleanor asked.

"She's got to," Otto reasoned. "She's not like Mr. January. He just popped in and made the Society do stuff, but she has a business. It's been around for ages. She can't drag all her makeup through mud holes to get around. She needs a place to store it, and to meet with people, and all sorts of things."

"Then we shall venture into the lair of the witch herself," Pip said. There was an awkward silence, and she cleared her throat. "We should go check that out," she amended.

"Do you think it's safe to go outside?" Eleanor asked.

"No. But what else are we going to do?" Pip replied. "We have to try."

THEY EXPLAINED THEIR plan to Jack, who wasn't happy but agreed to stay behind and protect Jenny and Naomi. That meant they had to take their bikes into town, but the way Jack drove it wouldn't be much slower than taking the car.

Outside of Ashford House, everything had turned gray. It wasn't just the setting of the sun—all the color was gone from the world, just like on Halloween. They moved in silence through the darkness, tensed for any sign of mucks.

At the edge of town they saw a car, its door wrenched open with giant claw marks along its side, the light still on and the interior coated in mud. The hazard lights were blinking.

"Whose car is that?" Eleanor asked.

"I don't know," Otto replied, shaking his head. They stayed there a moment, staring at the empty car. And then they started off again, their silence grim.

The offices were locked, but Pip had spent the last few months learning how to pick locks, and it took her only a few minutes to get them in. Inside it was black as a pit. They turned on their flashlights and ventured in.

It looked like a normal office. There were SixSeed-branded motivational posters on the walls and pictures of the stuff you could get for reaching big sales goals. Shelves along the walls held a treasure trove of products. Robbed of color, they looked glum and uninspiring.

"Back there," Pip said, pointing the flashlight. A door against the back wall was labeled KORRI PROSPER, REGIONAL REPRESENTATIVE.

This lock took a bit longer to spring. Eleanor kept watch, peering out of the windows at the darkened parking lot. Pip muttered to herself as she worked. Finally she cast a grin over her shoulder. "I SixSeeded," she declared, and pushed the door open.

Beyond the door, the gray of the world outside was gone. Korri Prosper's office was far bigger than it should have been, and its stone floor was so cold the chill seeped in through their feet. The walls were solid stone as well, almost like a natural cave except for the fact that they were so straight and even. Columns rose at the four corners of the room, smooth in the middle but turning into rough stalagmites at their bases. A huge stone desk rose right out of the floor in the center of the room, and behind it hung a framed painting.

"Is that the People Who Look Away?" Otto asked.

Eleanor shone her flashlight on the painting. It showed three figures facing away, two female and one male, but they seemed to be children. The girls had braids with strange purple flowers woven into them, and the boy wore a delicate iron circlet, like a crown.

Behind them stood two larger figures, tall and spindly, like people who had been stretched out. It seemed to be a man and a woman, but their bodies were so distorted it was hard to tell. They had their hands on the children's shoulders, and their fingers were long and thin like spider's legs. Their faces were gray and featureless except for their black, lidless eyes, which stared out from under jagged crowns.

"Family portrait?" Otto suggested.

Eleanor shuddered. "I don't think I want to meet Mom and Dad."

"Their kids are bad enough," Pip agreed. "Okay. Let's check out the desk."

"There's a bookshelf over here," Otto said, indicating the right-hand wall, and moved toward it.

Eleanor's flashlight beam moved over a shadow in the far corner. She frowned. It looked odd. Too deep. She walked toward it slowly. The shadowy patch was half-hidden by the nearest stone column, but as she moved sideways she saw it was in fact a stone passageway. "Look at this," she said, but Pip and Otto didn't seem to hear her. She glanced back. The figures in the painting had turned to watch her, but they were the only ones paying attention. Pip bent over a desk drawer. Otto knelt by the bookcase.

She should have been afraid, but she turned back toward the passageway and stepped into it. Her footsteps echoed as she moved deeper, and the smell of damp stone surrounded her. Still she kept onward, some inner voice compelling her forward.

The passageway twisted, and then opened up into a huge cavern. She didn't need her flashlight anymore. Thousands of glowing mushrooms spilled out across the cave floor, lighting everything in spectral blues and greens, and the water that trickled down the walls shimmered like the rain.

The entire cave was full of doors. There were iron doors and wooden doors, huge medieval doors carved with dragons and simple slabs of wood, doors with brass knockers and ornate keyholes. The mushrooms grew thickest around the bases of the doors, lending each an eerie spotlight.

Eleanor's flashlight beam fell across one of the simplest doors. Just wood with an iron handle. She stared at it, her heart beating fast. Something about it called to her. She took a tentative step forward, then another, aware that it didn't make sense, certain it was some kind of trap, but unable to resist.

Step by step, she approached the door. The dripping water kept a steadier tempo than her ragged breathing, falling in time to the ever-present clock. Her hand reached out and brushed the handle.

From the other side of the door came the faint sound of singing. Eleanor knew that song. She knew that *voice*.

"Mom!" she cried, and yanked open the door.

Twenty-Two

On the other side, an emerald forest glimmered with morning light. Thick moss carpeted the rolling ground, and blue and scarlet birds flickered between the branches. Eleanor plunged through, following the sound of the singing. It was coming from the other side of a small hill. She scrambled over it, nearly falling down the far side.

A deep stream wound between the trees just ahead of her, shadowed by the branches hanging over it. A woman stood in the middle of the stream, up to her waist in water. The woman had pale green skin and huge eyes and black hair that floated out around her on top of the water. She swayed in time to the singing of a woman who stood on the near shore, her brown hair bound in a braid.

"Mom!" Eleanor called again, and ran forward.

The green-skinned woman jerked. Her head whipped toward Eleanor. She opened her mouth, baring three rows of needle-fine teeth, and dived beneath the surface of the water. Eleanor caught a flash of rippling fins, and then she was gone. Eleanor's mother whirled as Eleanor pelted forward.

Eleanor flung her arms around her mother. "Mom! Where have you been? What happened to you? The house burned down and you were gone and the cat-of-ashes said—"

"Calm yourself, child," her mother said, and peeled Eleanor's arms away, pushing her gently but firmly back. She looked down at Eleanor with a mixture of puzzlement and distaste, and not one ounce of recognition.

Eleanor's whole body jolted with sudden cold. "Mom? It's me," she said.

It was her mother—almost exactly as she remembered her. Brown hair, held back in a long braid. Plain, strong features, a sharp nose and ears that stuck out a little. But Eleanor had never seen her mother in the dress she now wore, deep blue with moons and stars stitched around the cuffs and hems. And her mother's eyes were hazel, not slate gray, and had never looked at her like that. Like she didn't know Eleanor at all.

"Hedgewitch," Eleanor said softly, falling back a step.

"I am that," her mother said. "And you are?"

"Eleanor." Her voice was wooden. Her joy at seeing her mother withered and rotted in her chest.

"Well, Eleanor, these woods are very dangerous," the hedge-witch said, bending to pick up a leather satchel. "No place for a child, certainly, unless you wish to be the rusalka's next meal." She waved over her shoulder toward the stream.

"I heard you singing," Eleanor said faintly.

"A song for an enchanted river stone. It was a fair trade, but you interrupted," the hedgewitch said. "Where did you come from?"

"Just over the hill," Eleanor managed. She didn't recognize her at all.

"Through Prosper's door? How did you manage that?" the hedgewitch asked. She spoke like Eleanor's mother. She moved like her. But she wasn't her.

No. It couldn't be true. She had to recognize Eleanor. She had to recognize her own daughter. "Do you know me? At all?"

"Have we met, then?" the hedgewitch asked, not sounding terribly interested in the answer. "You should go back the way you came. Like I said, these woods aren't safe." She turned to go.

"Wait!" Eleanor cried.

The hedgewitch sighed. "I don't have time to shepherd lost children around," she said.

"But it's me. It's Eleanor," Eleanor said, and lunged forward, seizing her mother's hand. Her mother stared down at her.

"So you've said. But I don't know anyone by that name," she said.

"Yes, you do. I'm Eleanor and you're Claire. You're my mother," Eleanor said. "Remember. You have to remember. Please."

The hedgewitch extracted her hand from Eleanor's. "Look, child. I'm not your mother."

"I'm not lying."

"I didn't say that you were. Only that you are mistaken. I'm no one's mother, and I don't remember you."

"What about Jack?" Eleanor asked, tears in her voice. "Do you remember him, at least?"

"Do you know where he is?" the hedgewitch asked, head tilting to the side. "The world walker had no notion of where he'd gotten to."

"He's with us—with me. He was trapped in the Wickerwood, but we saved him, and now my friend is turning into the new Jack and—"

The hedgewitch grunted. "Then Jack is only partially manifested right now. That's inconvenient. Oh, well. I shall have to find him once he is fully written. As for you, I'm sorry about whatever connection you have to my prior self, but I am not she, and she is not me."

Eleanor searched those gray eyes for any sign of the mother she knew, but there was none. "Please," she whispered.

"Compassion is not part of my story, child," the hedgewitch said matter-of-factly.

Eleanor felt numb. Her mother was gone. She was really, truly gone. All this time she'd held onto the knowledge that her mother was out there somewhere. Even when she'd thought that she set the fire that nearly killed Eleanor, knowing she was alive had helped. But while this woman might look like Claire Barton, Claire Barton was dead.

Grief wrapped Eleanor in its soft arms, and whispered gently in her ear. She shut her eyes. Claire Barton was gone. And this was what was going to happen to Pip, too. She was going to stare out at Eleanor with blank gray eyes and not even know her name.

"Come now, child," the hedgewitch said. "Gather yourself and go."

Eleanor's eyes snapped open. Pip wasn't gone. Not yet. And neither were Ben, or Josephine, or any of the others. She had to be strong. Even if she had to do it alone. "Compassion might not be part of your story, but knowledge is," she said. Her voice shook, but it had steel. She couldn't fall apart, not now. Not with so many people counting on her.

Her mother might not be able to help her now. But maybe the hedgewitch could.

"True," the hedgewitch acknowledged, curiosity alight in her colorless eyes. "What do you wish to know?"

"Mrs. Prosper is kidnapping people for a ritual in the Wickerwood," Eleanor said. "Thirteen upside-down trees with people in them. What is the ritual for?"

"Mrs. Prosper and her siblings want only one thing. To open the door to the realm of their father, the Pallid King," the hedgewitch said. "There are a number of rituals that might do. What you describe is certainly one of them. Thirteen souls sacrificed in a place of beauty corrupted into evil—a ritual to open any door, that one included."

"But they're already turning thirteen-year-olds into keys

to open the door," Eleanor said. "Why would they need two rituals?"

"Because when that door opens, their parents are going to want to know which of them managed it. It pays to be the favorite child. And it is dangerous not to be," the hedgewitch said, eyes glinting.

"Mrs. Prosper doesn't want Mr. January getting the credit," Eleanor said, understanding at last. "She wants to do things her way."

"A plausible hypothesis, at least," the hedgewitch said. She waved to Eleanor, beckoning her to walk alongside her back up the hill. Eleanor could almost pretend she was walking with her mother, and that everything was all right. Almost. But she couldn't squelch the cold, slick horror of looking at her mother's face and seeing a stranger staring back.

"We need to stop her. But we don't know how," Eleanor said, forcing herself to focus.

"Another thing about the hedgewitch is that I don't like to give answers away for free," the witch said. "An answer for an answer. How did you find me?"

"I heard you singing through the door," Eleanor said, but that wasn't quite right, was it? She'd only heard the singing when she touched the handle. "Or. I don't know. I just knew I had to open it."

The hedgewitch seized her chin and tilted her face up, searching her eyes as if she expected to find something there. Her grip was firm, without an ounce of affection in it. "No," she murmured. "Or not yet, at least." She released Eleanor, who stumbled back, rubbing her cheek. "Tell Jack I look forward to seeing him, once he's himself again."

"Herself," Eleanor corrected quietly. "Pip's a girl."

"That will be a nice change of pace," the hedgewitch said, unconcerned. "You want to know how to defeat Mrs. Prosper. You can't. She is immortal, the same as her siblings. No weapon will harm them."

"We don't need to kill her. Just keep her from winning until after the equinox," Eleanor said. She frowned, thinking. "You said that the ritual could open any door, not just the one she wants to. In *Wickerwood*, they trap the witch in a world she can't escape. Could we change what door it's opening? Trick her into going somewhere else?"

"Mrs. Prosper walks between worlds as easily as you cross from one room to another," the hedgewitch said. "But some worlds are harder to navigate than others. It is possible that you might delay her."

Eleanor bit her lip. "Isn't there a labyrinth world? The endless labyrinth, or something?"

"There is," the hedgewitch replied approvingly.

"We read in a book about a mushroom that can open the way there," Eleanor said.

"*Gomphus labyrinthus.* If you can get your hands on it, and perform the proper counter-ritual, that might work," the hedgewitch said.

"What's the proper counter-ritual?"

"An answer for an answer, remember?" the hedgewitch said.

"Fine. What do you want to know?" Eleanor snapped. Her mother had never been cold like this, so unworried. She hated this woman with her gray eyes and her steady voice. Hated her for stealing her mother away, erasing her.

"I—" For the first time, the hedgewitch hesitated. And then she whispered, low and urgent, "Are you safe?"

For an instant, the gray of her eyes flickered, turning hazel. Or was it only a trick of the light?

Eleanor might have lied. Lying was easy. Lying was sometimes the kindest thing you could do. But this time, she told the truth. "No," she said. "But I'm fighting. And I'm not alone."

The hedgewitch nodded slowly. She reached into her satchel and drew out a piece of thick, yellowish paper and held it out to Eleanor. As soon as Eleanor's fingers closed around it, words began to write themselves on its surface.

To open the way to the endless maze, place the mushrooms at the points of greatest power and focus. Repeat the incantation until the rain begins to glow; they must be spoken from memory, or it will not work. Then the door will open, and anyone holding a labyrinthus mushroom will be pulled through.

The incantation was written below: *come wending, come wandering, those wishing to be lost . . .*

The words wrote themselves on and on, the incantation spilling out over the page.

"She must accept the mushroom willingly in order to be pulled through the door," the hedgewitch warned. "If you force it on her, it won't work."

"Thank you," Eleanor said.

"Be careful," the hedgewitch replied.

"I thought you didn't care," Eleanor said, hope the faintest flicker in her heart.

"It's good advice regardless," the hedgewitch said, and shrugged. "Now there's your door. Best get through before something in these woods gets hungry."

Eleanor nodded. And then, before the hedgewitch could stop her, she darted forward and wrapped her arms one more time around her mother. The hedgewitch stiffened. Then she lifted one hand, and stroked Eleanor's hair gently.

"Go on, Elle," she whispered.

Eleanor pulled away. The hedgewitch's face was already back to its expression of irritation and boredom, her eyes as gray as stone.

"Goodbye," Eleanor said. She forced herself to turn away and walked back through the door. She didn't let herself turn. If she didn't turn, she could imagine that those gray eyes had turned hazel one last time. That it was her mother watching her go, and wishing her safe.

The door shut behind her, and she was alone.

Twenty-Three

Eleanor stumbled out of the cave. The doors creaked and whispered behind her, calling to her to open them. They sounded hungry, and she did not want to find out what would happen if she lingered—or tried to open one.

Something had drawn her to her mother. She'd been meant to find her. Eleanor told herself that must mean that there was still hope to save her, and she tucked that kindly lie deep inside herself.

Pip and Otto were talking frantically when she emerged from the hallway.

"She didn't leave. We would have seen her leave!" Otto said.

"Then where *is* she?" Pip demanded.

"Here," Eleanor said. They spun, startled, and Pip half drew Gloaming before relaxing.

"Where did you go?" Otto asked.

"I was right—" Eleanor turned. The hallway was gone. The corner was just a corner. "There was a passageway there."

Otto went to press his hands against the stone, but it didn't budge. Eleanor shivered. What if she'd gotten trapped in there?

"Did you find anything?" Pip asked.

Eleanor swallowed. "Yeah," she said, voice hoarse. "I think I know how to beat Mrs. Prosper."

She took a deep breath, and she told them everything. It took a few tries to get through it all, and she almost broke into tears more than once. But at last she was done, and Pip and Otto stared at her with wide eyes.

"I'm so sorry, Eleanor," Otto said.

She shook her head. "I don't want to talk about it. Let's save ourselves, and then we're going to save her."

"Is that even possible?" Pip asked. She wasn't just asking for Eleanor's mother.

"It has to be," Eleanor said firmly. Even if it was too late for her mother, it couldn't be too late for Pip. She was *Pip*. She was right here. She was still her, and she was going to stay that way.

But first they had to stay alive.

"Let's get back to Jack," Eleanor said. "I've got a plan. Or most of one. But we're all going to need to help."

They filed back out of the room. At the doorway Eleanor paused and looked once more at the portrait on the far wall.

The looming monarchs glared down at her with their strange, black eyes.

The male figure's hand rose slowly from where it had rested on the young January's shoulder. One clawed fingertip tapped three times against the surface of the painting, as if it was nothing more than a pane of glass—and might shatter.

Eleanor slammed the door shut and ran to catch up.

ELEANOR DIDN'T RELAX until they'd slammed the door of the secret room shut behind them. Jenny had fallen asleep with Naomi curled up in her arms, snoring her little baby snores. Jack joined them toward the back of the room where they wouldn't disturb Jenny and Naomi, and Eleanor explained what had happened. This time she kept her voice level, no emotion in it. Jack listened gravely, and when she was done he looked away for a long moment.

"I was already Jack when I fell in love with Claire. Because of that, I have been able to hold on to that love. It isn't the same for Claire. If she is gone . . ." He trailed off and cleared his throat. "What Claire would want is for her daughter to be safe. Tell us this plan of yours, Eleanor."

Eleanor nodded. Her voice was shaky as she began, but grew stronger as she spoke. "Mrs. Prosper is cheating. She isn't doing what she agreed to. She's doing her own ritual instead. Which means that she lied to Mr. January. She's sneaking around behind his back."

"I don't think Mr. January would like that very much," Otto said.

Pip yawned. "Whatever. Just tell me when I get to poke her with Gloaming."

Eleanor frowned at her. Pip always joked around about being only good for hitting things, but this seemed more dismissive than usual. She really looked bored. "You can't," she said. "Like it says in *Wickerwood*, weapons can't hurt her."

"Well, that's not fair," Otto objected. "How are we supposed to beat her?"

"Everything we need to know is in the books. It just took my mom—the hedgewitch—to help me put it all together," Eleanor said. She set the three books out next to each other on the floor. *Wickerwood*, *Practical Mycology*, and *Thirteen Tales of the Gray*.

"In *Wickerwood*, they trap her in another world," Pip said.

"Exactly," Eleanor said, nodding.

"And the labyrinth mushroom opens a door to a maze world," Otto added. Eleanor smiled. They were getting it.

"The hedgewitch gave me a spell we can use. But it's complicated," Eleanor said. She handed the paper to Otto. Pip peered over his shoulder.

"We're going to need the mushrooms, for one thing," Otto pointed out. "They only grow in Wales."

Pip nodded. "And we're going to need one heck of a distraction if we're going to recite all of this without getting tackle-hugged by mucks."

"I think we can manage both those things," Eleanor said slowly. "But it requires getting help from the cat-of-ashes."

She explained her idea carefully, figuring it out as she spoke. And when she was done, she bit her lip. "What do you think?"

"I think you're right," Pip said.

"So what does that mean?" Otto asked.

"It means we have a way to win," Eleanor replied. Otto's forehead creased—and then he nodded. And so did Pip.

"We also need to get into the Wickerwood. And you shut Jack's mudhole," Otto said.

"We need a muck to open one. And we need bait," Eleanor said.

"I'm not being bait. I've got Gloaming," Pip said. "You'll need me to fight the mucks."

"I have to recite the spell," Otto added.

"I could do it," Eleanor said nervously.

"Absolutely not," Jack said.

"I can do it," Eleanor insisted.

"You three need each other," Jack said gently. "And my usefulness is fading along with the story. I will be the bait in your trap."

"Are you sure?" Eleanor asked. "I—"

"It is the least I can do for you three," Jack said. *You three*, not just *you*. Eleanor couldn't help being a little bit disappointed at that.

"Then let's get started," she said. "We have a lot to do."

Twenty-Four

Eleanor walked through the orchard slowly, arms crossed tight against the chill. The trees creaked in the breeze under a light patter of rain. There was no moon tonight, and the lights of the house were the only thing pushing against the darkness. Eleanor could barely distinguish the tops of the trees of the forest from the black clouds. "Cat?" she called softly. "Cat-of-ashes? Are you here? Are you watching?"

The cat melted out of the shadows, prancing forward with little sparks swirling out from under her paws. "Careful. I don't like coming when I'm called," she said, purring, and stood a short distance away, the tip of her tail twitching back and forth.

"I know. I'm sorry. But I need your help," Eleanor said.

"Sorry. All out of helpfulness," the cat-of-ashes said, and started to turn away.

"Wait! Mr. January is going to want to hear this." That gave the cat pause. She looked expectantly at Eleanor, and Eleanor wetted her lips. "Mrs. Prosper is cheating."

"We've covered that. Mr. January isn't interested in interfering beyond sending me."

"But it's not just that she jumped the gun," Eleanor said. "She's not trying to catch us at all. She's doing a different ritual. She's trying to open the door all by herself."

The cat-of-ashes' eyes narrowed. "Now that *is* interesting. But what proof do you have?"

"I saw it. A ritual with thirteen trees in the Wickerwood." She couldn't bring herself to mention her mother.

"Humans lie," the cat-of-ashes said. "You break promises and ignore rules and nothing happens to you whatsoever. He won't take your word for it."

"Then come with us. We'll show you," Eleanor said desperately.

"I'll pass along the message," the cat-of-ashes said. "But if you're putting all your hopes on my master to save you—"

"We're not," Eleanor replied. "And that's why I need your help. *Your* help, not his."

"I see. And what kind of help would that be?" the cat-of-ashes asked.

"You have special ways of getting around," Eleanor said. "Right? You went straight through my window on Halloween, and you appear with Mr. January. How fast can you travel?"

"It's not a matter of fast," the cat-of-ashes said. "It's a matter of knowing the hidden ways. Where do you want me to go?"

She was curious now. That was good. She might not do anything out of the goodness of her heart, but a cat couldn't resist curiosity. No wonder she and the hedgewitch got along.

"Well," Eleanor said, "have you ever been to Wales?"

ELEANOR SAT ON a stump while she waited for the others. Pip was the first to appear, jogging up and pulling her hair into a tight ponytail as she went. "Found it," she said. She pulled the little pot of mud mask out of her pocket and flashed it at Eleanor. "Is Miss Kitty going to play along?"

"I think so," Eleanor said, getting to her feet. She held up her hand, revealing the dirty handkerchief there, tied around lumpy contents. She bit her lip. "Pip. Maybe it's better—maybe you should stay," she said.

Pip's eyes flashed with annoyance. "You're not leaving me behind."

"But the Story—"

"Is a good thing, Eleanor. I can be useful now," Pip said. She rested her hand on Gloaming's hilt and grinned. "Come on. I've got a sword. How cool is that?"

"It's going to change you," Eleanor said.

Pip's smile faltered, but then she shrugged. "So? No big loss."

Eleanor stared at her. "Don't say that."

"You and Otto are the smart ones. The best I can do is hit

things, and there's a reason my nickname used to be Pipsqueak. I'm not big or strong or tough, but with Gloaming I can be. I can be the Jack, and I can be worth something," Pip said.

"I just found you and Otto. I can't lose you," Eleanor said desperately, and she grabbed Pip's hand. "I don't care if you have a sword or if you're strong or tough. You're amazing, Pip, *you* are."

But Pip pulled her hand away, shaking her head. Her voice dropped to a fragile whisper. "It doesn't matter, Eleanor. We can't stop it."

And then Eleanor saw it in her eyes: fear. Pip was afraid. But being angry was easier, and so was being fierce.

"It feels good," Pip confessed. "I can sort of—hear it. The Prime Story. Almost like words. And it's simple. The Jack isn't scared or sad. It's fierce and it's brave and I want that, Eleanor. I want to know what to feel and what to do."

Eleanor didn't know what to say. She couldn't speak at all. Her throat had closed up around a big, painful lump, and tears pricked at her eyes. She couldn't lose Pip. She *couldn't*. She wished they'd left Jack in those woods, that Pip had never lifted Gloaming out of the mud.

"I found them!" Otto declared at that moment, jogging up from the direction of the forest, his backpack bulging and mud streaking his clothes. "You guys all set?"

Eleanor blinked furiously to clear her eyes of tears. "We're good," she said, just as Jack joined them, carrying the set of stick charms to hold the passageway open.

"Yeah, all set," Pip said. She gave Eleanor a warning look—a "we're done talking about this" look.

"Are you sure about this?" Otto asked Jack. "We could figure something else out."

"It is a sound strategy," Jack said. Eleanor could hear the nervousness in his voice. Now that the story had left him, the marvelous healing he had wouldn't help him if he got hurt.

"Right." Pip scrunched her hands into fists, then relaxed them, over and over. "Are we ready, then?"

"Ready as we're going to get," Otto replied.

Pip held out the jar of SixSeed ReJubilation Mushroom-Boosted Mud Mask, shut tightly, which she'd gotten from upstairs. Jack took it, handing off the charms to Pip.

"Hide yourselves," he said. They nodded and spread out across the orchard, crouching in the shadows of the gnarled apple trees. His edges barely lit with the lights from the house, Jack unscrewed the jar and scooped up a bit on his fingers. He smeared it over his cheeks and neck, slathering it on heavily. They wanted to make sure the mucks would come.

And then they waited. Seconds stretched into minutes. Eleanor's thighs and knees started to hurt from crouching so long, and still Jack just stood there. Waiting. Maybe they were done collecting people. Maybe they didn't need any more.

Eleanor strained to hear shuffling or the crunch of a big footstep, but she'd forgotten how quiet the mucks were. When it came, it was silent, rising from the ground thirty feet from Jack. Behind him.

If it grabbed him, it would drag him right into the mud pit, and there was no guarantee they could jump in after him before it closed the passage. "Look out!" Eleanor yelled.

Jack didn't stand and fight. He bolted. He was weak. Slow. A few strides and the muck would be on him, but they couldn't stop to help or even to worry about him. Pip, Eleanor, and Otto sprinted for the spot where the muck had emerged.

Pip jammed the upside-down charm into the dirt and dived right in, not even hesitating. Eleanor jammed her eyes shut, plugged her nose, and jumped into the mud feetfirst.

The extra momentum seemed to slurp her through faster than before, and she heaved herself up to semisolid ground only a few seconds later, just behind Pip, who was already driving the second charm into the mud. Otto took a little longer and came up coughing, but they pulled him to his feet and ran full tilt toward the nearest tree. They skidded behind it and dropped down, trying to keep their breathing quiet in the gloom—just in time.

The muck emerged a few moments later, Jack's limp form draped over his shoulder. Eleanor's breath hissed between her teeth. Pip put a hand on her shoulder. "It was the only way to get here," she reminded her.

The muck moved off far too quickly to follow, disappearing into the dusk-like darkness of the Wickerwood. Otto pulled out his compass, which he'd gotten from Bartimaeus's collection.

Instead of showing north, south, east, and west, it had a thorny vine at one end and a blue rose at the other. The rose meant safety, the thorn meant danger.

They turned until the compass pointed firmly toward the thorns. It was the direction the muck had gone.

They moved as quickly as the sucking mud would allow them. It wasn't long before they didn't need the compass at all. Up ahead, spectral lights glowed, illuminating the circle of trees. The lights hung in their upturned roots. As the trio grew closer, they could see that the lights were glowcaps, but massive.

Mucks surrounded the circle of trees, unnaturally still. The hollows of the trees were packed with mud, encasing the standing forms of everyone Mrs. Prosper had taken. Their faces stuck out, so at least they could breathe. At least they were alive. Eleanor spotted Pip's dad and Jack on the far side, Susannah Chen next to them.

Then there was a new figure in the circle. Mrs. Prosper didn't step into the light—she wasn't there, and then she was. But she had changed. Gone was the blazer and pencil skirt. She looked the way she had when they saw her in the gray world: tall and thin, almost bony, her hair clapped back in a tight bun, a gray dress fluttering against the muddy ground. She didn't sink into the mud; she stood on top of it, as if she didn't weigh anything at all.

She was facing away from them. This was her true self.

She stepped forward—but moved backward. Eleanor's head

hurt as her mind tried to comprehend it. Mrs. Prosper moved into the center of the circle and raised her hands.

"Thirteen I have gathered," she said. Her voice was like leaves scuttling over dry ground. "I have prepared this place with darkness and with death. With creeping curses and despair. And now these thirteen lives will flow into the pit, and the mouth of the next world shall open."

The mucks began to sing. It was a horrid, hollow sound, all moan and tremble, and they swayed with it. Eleanor felt rooted to the spot, transfixed.

No. No, they had to move. They had to move *now*. For Ben. For Aunt Josephine. For all of them. No more planning. Time for doing.

She ran forward, bursting into the light with a yell.

"Stop!" she cried. "We changed our minds."

Mrs. Prosper's hands dropped. The mucks fell silent. Her head tilted to the side, as if she was examining Eleanor. "Changed your minds?"

"Yeah," Eleanor said. She heard Otto and Pip squishing up behind her, moving now that Mrs. Prosper's ritual had stopped. Or paused, at least. "About your deal. We agree. We'll give ourselves to you if you let everybody go. But you have to let them go *first*. That way we know you aren't lying."

"I see," Mrs. Prosper said. She didn't move.

"So?" Otto asked. "Go ahead. Let everybody go."

Mrs. Prosper's hands twitched, and for one moment Eleanor thought they'd gotten it wrong. That she would let everyone go, and take the three of them, and that would be that. Defeat. But there was a long moment of silence, and Mrs. Prosper sighed. She turned slowly to face them. "I'm disappointed. I thought you were made of sterner stuff."

"Well, we're not. Let's get this over with," Eleanor said. "Or do you just want to hang around until sunset and lose your chance?"

"I am through with waiting," Mrs. Prosper said. She started to raise her hands again, and Eleanor and the others exchanged a frantic glance. If she just went ahead with the ritual, this wouldn't work.

"Are you scared or something?" Pip asked. "I bet she's scared."

"I think she's just mad her plan didn't work," Otto said with a shrug, catching on. "I mean, she did all that mudnapping and we kind of made fun of her."

Mrs. Prosper gave a low chuckle. "You foolish children," she said. "I never expected you to accept. I knew you would refuse. And I expected you to stumble your way in here, playing at being heroes. My beasts are more than ready to handle you, should you try to interfere, but I don't need you."

"I don't get it," Pip said, scratching her chin. "Were you that sure you couldn't win the bet with your brother?"

"No!" Mrs. Prosper snapped. "I never had any intention of entrapping you, because it is a ridiculous idea in the first place. Three children every thirteen years. Yes, it has poetry. Yes, it has power. But so many points of failure. I should never have agreed to let my brother make the attempt in the first place. My plan is far more direct. The Wickerwood's curse provides plenty of power."

"I still don't understand," Otto said. "How is this a better plan? I mean, Mr. January's just about done. So it seems like his stuff's working fine."

"And I could have finished and had the door open a century ago if I hadn't had to hide what I was doing. But he insisted that we stay *focused*. So we agreed: we would see his plan through before we made any other attempts. We *promised*." She sounded disgusted with herself. "But I told you, I don't like to take chances. I knew we needed a backup plan in case his went wrong."

More like she wanted to show him up, Eleanor thought, but she didn't say it out loud.

"I worked quietly. Subtly. Gathering one person at a time from Eden Eld over the course of years. Of a *century*. And then I was ready—far sooner than my brother, I might add. But *he* ruined it all." She stabbed her finger in Jack's direction. "Breaking free while I was preoccupied. It won't happen again."

"Wait. How come it took you a century to get thirteen people before, but you could grab them all at once this time?" Eleanor asked, layering her voice with deep confusion.

Mrs. Prosper chuckled. "My brother's inability to pass up a wager gave me the perfect opportunity to complete my own project. I had to hide my efforts from my siblings all this time, but now I have the perfect excuse. Kidnapping people? Oh, it's just part of this new bargain of yours, dear brother. To lure the children into the trap for you. He thinks I'm playing by his rules, and all the while I'm playing him for a fool."

"I see. So, to be very, very clear. You're cheating. You're breaking the rules. You're just pretending to try and get the three of us like you agreed to. Instead, you're kidnapping people to do a ritual you promised you wouldn't do. Is that right?"

"More or less. Now stand back. If you don't interfere, I won't have my beasts tear you apart." She began to lift her hands.

"Do you think that's enough?" Eleanor asked loudly.

"Oh, plenty," the cat-of-ashes said.

Twenty-Five

The cat-of-ashes slinked out from around a tree. The heat of her paws dried the mud beneath her, letting her skip along the surface, but she still shook her paws with every step and made a disgusted face before leaping up into the roots of one of the snags.

"Horrid beast. What are you doing here?" Mrs. Prosper asked.

"Keeping an eye on you. Which apparently I should have been doing a lot more of," the cat-of-ashes said, examining her claws.

"If you think you are going to scurry off and rat to your master—"

"Me? *Rat?* Watch your language," the cat hissed.

"My servants will turn you into so much ragged fur and jagged bone," Mrs. Prosper threatened.

The cat-of-ashes let out an exaggerated yawn. "Oh, how

frightening. I'm terrified, really. Very well. I won't go any-where. I'll just sit here."

Mrs. Prosper's silence was full of sharp points. "A deal, then. Your silence in exchange for . . . what, exactly?"

"Ugh, deals. No. You really think I'd reveal myself before I'd already sent word?" the cat-of-ashes asked, blinking her big green eyes.

At that moment, the air filled with a terrible *clackclack-clack* that Eleanor knew well. The rattlebird. It swooped down through the trees, alighting on another of the uprooted snags, and folded its ragged wings around its body.

"Oathbreaker. Cheat. Liar," it croaked.

"Shouldn't have done that," rumbled another voice, and the graveyard dog, black and hulking, crept into view. A growl rattled its massive chest as smoke trickled from between its teeth.

"You are puppets and playthings. You don't frighten me," Mrs. Prosper scoffed.

"But I should," Mr. January said. In the same way she had appeared, simply *there*, so did he. He stood between the three of them and Mrs. Prosper, facing the children. When he'd spoken to them a few days ago, his voice had been full of mirth and amusement. Now it simmered with anger.

He turned away to look directly at his sister, and Eleanor had a momentary flash of sympathy for her. They had been fixed with that gaze before, the one he chose when he truly turned his attention to you. It wasn't a comfortable thing at all.

The two circled each other, Mr. January twirling his cane. Mrs. Prosper's hands curled into fists.

"Let me finish," Mrs. Prosper said. "What does it matter whose scheme succeeds? The door will be open. We will be able to go home."

"It matters because we agreed," Mr. January said. "And if all that mattered was getting home, you would have thrown yourself into acquiring those three lovely little treasures, not trying to prove your way was better."

"It *is* better," Mrs. Prosper snapped.

The mucks hadn't moved. Eleanor edged toward the circle of them, getting as close as she dared. They didn't seem to even be looking at anything in particular—they just stood stock-still, gazing off into the distance.

"I don't think they'll do anything unless she commands them," she whispered. "We'd better move now."

Pip and Otto nodded their agreement. Otto slung the backpack off his shoulder and unzipped it. Five dormant glimmermanders were piled inside, looking undamaged by their inelegant transportation. Tucked in next to them were water bottles filled with the oil mixture. They traded: Eleanor giving him the handkerchief with the supplies the cat-of-ashes had fetched, Eleanor and Pip dividing the glimmermanders and oil between them.

"Split up. I'll start with Jack," Pip said.

Mr. January and Mrs. Prosper had stopped circling each other, stopped talking. They stared into each other's eyes, and the air bent and warped weirdly around them. They seemed utterly oblivious to anything happening around them.

Good.

Eleanor grabbed a water bottle and a glimmermander and scurried to the nearest tree. She came around and felt a flutter of relief—April. She'd half feared she'd find a stranger in her place, April discarded somewhere in the forest. "You're awful," she told the unconscious girl. "But also, sorry this happened." She tried to pry April free, but the mud held her tight. Eleanor started scooping out double handfuls of mud until April sagged forward.

"Tricks," the rattlebird muttered, peering down between the roots above her.

"Oh, stuff it, featherbutt," said the cat-of-ashes.

Eleanor ignored them. Mr. January and Mrs. Prosper were still doing . . . whatever they were doing. Eleanor swiped the mud from April's face and smeared some of the oil mixture in its place, and then put the glimmermander on her chest.

She held her breath until the glow lit the glimmermander's skin and April's eyes fluttered open. Then April gasped and sat up. Her eyes went to the mucks, and she opened her mouth to scream, but Eleanor clamped a hand over it. "Not a sound. Can you stand? Walk?"

April nodded furiously and silently.

"Then help me," Eleanor said. She snagged the glimmermander before it could scurry away and moved on to the next tree.

Ben was inside. Eleanor's heart squeezed in her chest, but she didn't let herself slow down. She and April dug the mud out from around him, April whimpering quietly but never flagging. Eleanor couldn't help but be a little bit impressed. She hadn't even asked what was going on, she just helped.

Eleanor had just set the glimmermander—significantly squirmier now that it was awake—on her uncle's chest when Mr. January shouted in anger.

Eleanor whirled. Mr. January had been knocked back against one of the trees, and Mrs. Prosper stood with her hands like claws in the air, weird light flickering around her. Her breath hissed between her teeth. Her hair had come loose from its bun, hanging messily around her gaunt, gray-tinged face.

"Get them," she ordered. The mucks surged forward.

Pip drew her sword. The cat-of-ashes leaped, the graveyard dog lunged, the rattlebird dived, and everything erupted into chaos as mucks charged and Pip started swinging. The sword sliced and stabbed and swung, almost like it was doing the moving and she was just being dragged along with it. Milky white blood slicked the blade, coating her arms, but the mucks kept coming.

Eleanor cast her gaze around. Jack was helping Pip's dad to his feet and waving one arm, pointing off between the trees with the other. "Follow Jack!" Eleanor shouted. She ran from person to person—Pip had managed to wake two people as well, and Jack had pitched in, freeing seven victims. More than half. It was something, at least.

She grabbed Ben's arm and hauled him toward Jack. He stumbled blearily beside her. But as she reached the edge of the circle, the mucks cinched close around the crowd of dazed survivors, blocking their retreat.

And then Pip was there. She drove her fist, gripping Gloaming's hilt, into the nose of a muck with a *splunch* that was much softer and meatier than Eleanor expected. Pip danced past and swung wildly. Gloaming caught the light from the glowcaps and seemed to throw it at the mucks, sending them hooting and roaring and stumbling. "Go!" Pip roared, all fury and grace.

Otto yelled. Pip and Eleanor spun. Otto was at the edge of the circle of trees, and one of the mucks was advancing on him.

"Jack will help them. Let's go," Pip shouted. She and Eleanor sprinted back toward Otto. Pip went after the muck. Eleanor skidded to a halt next to Otto.

"What can I do?" she asked.

He thrust a pair of fleshy mushrooms into her hands. They had thick white stalks and caps like vases, filled in with the winding walls of mazes. *Gomphus labyrinthus.* "One left. That tree," he said, pointing. He sounded a bit out of breath, and as she hurried toward the tree he'd pointed at, she heard him muttering under his breath. *"Twist and tangle, briar and bramble . . ."*

Eleanor set the mushroom at the base of the tree, at the feet of one of the SixSeed party guests, still slumbering. *We'll get you out soon*, she promised silently, and then she stole back to Otto. Pip was with him, holding off the mucks each time they tried to advance. He stood with his eyes fixed on the center of the circle, muttering and swaying a little bit.

Whatever strange battle the brother and sister were locked in stilled. They broke apart, and Mr. January rolled his shoulders. "Well," he declared. "That was diverting." Eleanor's heart beat fast. If either of them noticed what the kids were up to—

"More time," Otto whispered.

"Your ritual is over," Eleanor yelled, striding forward and a bit to the side. "You don't have enough people. You lost."

The wood seemed to go still. The mucks—the ones still standing, of which there weren't that many—settled back on their haunches. The cat-of-ashes crouched, tail lashing, at the base of a tree, while the rattlebird circled overhead. The grave-yard dog stood at his master's side, and Mr. January himself straightened, brushing mud off his jacket.

"She's right," Mr. January said. "Your plan has come to nothing, sister."

"I still have them," Mrs. Prosper said, jabbing a finger in the trio's direction as Eleanor and Otto came to stand next to Pip. Eleanor put a hand on Pip's shoulder. She could feel Pip's muscles quivering under her palm.

"I think not," Mr. January replied. "You broke the rules of the bargain. You went after them before sunset—I imagine you thought it would be convenient to have them out of the way, even if you didn't actually want them—and you pursued a different goal entirely. Perhaps our sister will have better discipline."

Eleanor held her breath. Maybe Mr. January's appearance would be enough after all.

"It will still work," Mrs. Prosper said. "Fine, my plan failed. But I would rather be a failure at home than stranded out here. Let us finish your ritual, brother. There is still time, and our parents are waiting for us."

Mr. January was silent, considering. "It is my victory."

"Don't worry. I will make that very clear," she said. "Now if I may continue?"

Mr. January considered, then waved a hand. "Very well, carry on."

Of course it wasn't going to be that easy. Eleanor glanced at Otto. He was still muttering, but they were out of time.

Eleanor scurried over to Pip. "Pip. Here, quick, find somewhere to hide this," she hiss-whispered, and shoved the last *labyrinthus* mushroom toward her, blocking Mrs. Prosper's view with her body.

"What is that?" Mrs. Prosper demanded, before Pip could take it.

Eleanor swung around. "Nothing," she said, a little too high-pitched. She swallowed. "It's nothing." She kept the mushroom hidden behind her back.

"Come here," Mrs. Prosper said, scowling, and crooked a finger toward her.

"It's nothing, it's not important," Eleanor stammered.

"Come *here*," Mrs. Prosper said in a voice that echoed through the wood. "Or she will suffer the consequences."

She crooked a finger, and the nearest tree disgorged a waterfall of mud—and Aunt Josephine toppled out and staggered, coming awake as Mrs. Prosper's fingers raked through the air in strange movements. She stumbled over to Mrs. Prosper, who set a hand around the back of her neck and squeezed.

"Now come give me whatever it is you're hiding, or I will end her," Mrs. Prosper growled. Pip was shaking like she could barely stop herself from charging forward with Gloaming. But Gloaming couldn't help.

"All right," Eleanor said quickly. "All right." She inched forward slowly. She could barely hear Otto muttering feverishly.

"Over road and over flood, in the breath and in the blood . . ."

And then he gave a short, startled gasp. She didn't dare turn around. She kept her eyes fixed on Mrs. Prosper and crept forward another step.

A glimmering raindrop fell on Mrs. Prosper's shoulder.

"Show me what you have," Mrs. Prosper demanded.

"Let Aunt Josephine go," Eleanor said, voice wobbling. "And I promise I'll give it to you. And we'll go with you and— and—" She sucked in a blubbery, tear-filled breath.

"Oh, fine," Mrs. Prosper snarled. She shoved Aunt Josephine hard. Josephine went staggering and Pip ran to grab her, drag her out of the circle. "Now give it to me."

Eleanor whimpered, soft and helpless, and held out the dirty handkerchief wrapped around the last of the *labyrinthus* mushrooms. She stayed just a little bit too far back for Mrs. Prosper to reach.

Behind Mrs. Prosper, Mr. January took a large step backward. And then another for good measure.

Mrs. Prosper snatched the bundle from Eleanor's hands and flung aside the handkerchief. Her eyes fixed on the mushroom. "No," she said in horror.

Eleanor Barton might not be a genius or a warrior with a magical sword, but she was an *excellent* liar.

A rushing, slurping, sucking sound filled the air. The mud heaved beneath Eleanor's feet. Mrs. Prosper lunged for her— but her feet seemed stuck in place. She'd started to sink. The mud was up to her ankles now. She flung the mushroom away. "You little liar," she said, sounding both furious and somewhat amused.

"It's like what you said about makeup," Eleanor said. "We choose the way we look and the story we tell about ourselves by choosing what other people see. I made you see a helpless, frightened girl. But I'm not. I'm not afraid of you. I'm not afraid of your curse. Because I'm not just a scared little girl, I'm a scared girl with friends, and we're going to win *every time*." She was shouting now. "I'm not alone," she finished, her voice ragged and triumphant.

The mud began to open up under Mrs. Prosper's feet—and she began to laugh. "You think you have your friends, Eleanor Barton, and you think you'll have them forever. But you won't. One look in their eyes is enough to see that."

And then the mud parted, revealing a strange and twisting emptiness. Mrs. Prosper fell into it with a shriek. The mud slipped under Eleanor's feet, and she felt it dragging her toward that horrible hole—

But a hand grabbed her by the back of the collar and heaved her back, dragging her swiftly beyond the trees.

She got her feet under her and twisted, expecting to see Jack or Ben or even Pip, but she was staring up into the gray eyes of Mr. January. He tutted at her. "Now, now. I have use for you yet, and getting yourself lost in the maze won't do anyone any good," he informed her. He straightened his jacket.

In the circle, the mud closed up with a slushy *plop*. Eleanor backed away from Mr. January quickly, scurrying back to Pip and Otto, but he just chuckled.

"You three took quite the risk, calling on me. You are a delightfully entertaining lot. Really. It's inconvenient, but still—maybe it's for the best. The greater the challenge, the greater the power we'll claim when we win. And we'll need all the power we can get."

"Good for you," Eleanor said. "So what are you going to do to us now?"

"Alas. Nothing. Not right now. It isn't my day," Mr. January said, spreading his hands helplessly. "And I can't very well leave you here, or you'll be no fit snack for the curse when my time does roll around again." He sounded like he was sniffing something rotten. "So. Go on. Toddle along." He waggled his fingers.

"Not without all the people she took," Eleanor said.

"Don't get greedy," he advised, a warning tone in his voice.

"That's not greedy, it's just being a good person! It's like the bare minimum!" Otto declared. He and Pip moved to join Eleanor, presenting a scowling and united front to Mr. January.

"They're only here because your sister was cheating. And we beat her, so it's fair we get them back safe," Pip pointed out.

"Be careful with fair. It doesn't always favor the side of good," Mr. January warned.

"We were playing your sister's game. And rescuing them was the prize," Eleanor said. "Isn't that right? We won. And winner takes all. So they come with us."

His jaw tightened and his eyes narrowed, like he was trying to think of a way around this logic. "Fine," he said at last, waving a hand dismissively. "It's not as if I had any use for them. Take them and go. I shall open the door for you."

"Wait," Otto said. He tugged on Eleanor's arm. "The fernfolk," he whispered.

Eleanor glanced around the circle of trees. A few of the mucks were still standing, but more than a few were just lumps in the mud. She swallowed. "Your sister cursed this place, didn't she?" she asked.

"Indeed she did. Once it was a place of light and beauty, all green with ferns, but she shut out the sun and turned it to this ruin," Mr. January said.

"If we won, then—then lift the curse," Eleanor said. "We want them, too."

Mr. January smiled a patient smile. "Such soft, kind hearts you have. But as we have our seasons, so do heroes. And the season that might have saved the brackenfolk has long since ended." He gestured, a liquid movement that rippled out from his shoulder to the tips of his fingers.

The nearest muck shuddered. Mud slid from it, sloughing off all at once.

Beneath the mud was fur—shaggy fur clinging to tattered, leathery skin, which hung from bones that showed through here and there. A curve of rib, a knob of shoulder blade, a cracked kneecap. And in the splits and seams of its ragged hide grew something fleshy, something pale.

Mushrooms.

Their eyes. Those strangely dry eyes, without the wetness eyes normally had. They weren't eyes at all. They were mushroom caps.

Eleanor stumbled back, a horrified cry in her throat, and Mr. January laughed. It was a low, dry chuckle, and it made every hair on her arms stand on end.

"Their story is over, and it ended poorly. As will yours."

Eleanor felt sick. The mucks, the brackenbeasts—they were dead. Had been the whole time. No more songs and sunlight. This place would never be restored. The curse had won, and won forever.

She'd started to feel as if they were destined to win. As if they would always somehow eke out a victory, because that was the way stories were supposed to go. But not every story had a happy ending.

Theirs might not, either.

Mr. January twirled his cane, pointed it. Hinges creaked, and a door that had not been there a moment ago opened in the woods. On the other side, the sun was rising over the pines of Eden Eld. "You'll meet my other sister soon, children. And then it will be my turn again." He smiled broadly. "Assuming you defeat her. And I believe you will find her a much more focused opponent." He tipped his hat to them—and vanished.

The mucks stood, silent and still. The rain dripped down.

The Wickerwood remained in darkness.

Twenty-Six

The cat-of-ashes fetched back Jack and the others, though not without several complaints about "fetching" being for dogs, and they got the rest of Mrs. Prosper's victims roused and out Mr. January's door before the sun was too high in the sky. When the last person came stumbling through, the door slammed shut behind her and vanished.

It had left them in the field behind Eden Eld Academy. Everyone blinked and gazed around in confusion. Eleanor peered at their faces, trying to read what was going on behind them. Wondering if any of them would avoid the forgetting, and remember what had just happened to them.

One woman laughed brightly, waved a cheery farewell, and practically skipped off toward town, apparently deciding that this had been a normal lark that left her muddy and on foot in the middle of a field. More wandered away more slowly, vague expressions on their faces. A couple stumbled, muttering to themselves and shaking their heads firmly, and Eleanor was certain that however much they remembered now, they'd have forgotten it by the time they got home.

In the end there were four left. Mr. Maughan, Aunt Josephine, Ben, and Pip's dad. Everyone stood silently for a while. Mr. Maughan was squinting, and Eleanor remembered he'd lost his glasses. Pip's father was tending to Josephine, who still seemed rather more dazed than the rest of them. And Ben, after confirming with Eleanor that Jenny and the baby were okay, just sat in his bathrobe with his feet out in front of him, staring at nothing.

"Excuse me," Aunt Josephine said finally. Her voice was quiet, but it still shattered the silence like a ringing gong. Their heads snapped toward her, and she stammered a bit. "We just got kidnapped by monsters? Right? I didn't imagine that?"

"Don't be absurd. Monsters aren't real," Pip's father said. He paused. "Are they?"

"Pretty sure those were monsters," Ben intoned, sounding about a million miles away.

"There's a rational explanation," Pip's dad said. He looked at his daughter, a frown creasing his lips.

If he couldn't remember this, Eleanor realized, he wouldn't remember Pip—would he? When the Jack took her over, she would be not-Pip. A not-quite-Wrong Thing. And she would forget him, too.

"Absolutely," Pip said. "There's a rational explanation for *all* of it."

Her dad smiled. "What did I tell you?" he asked. "Goodness, I'm famished. We're a quick jaunt from the house. Why don't you all come over for some breakfast?"

"We'll be right over," Pip promised.

"I'll get the kettle on." He started off, muttering to himself about swamp gas.

"I'm forgetting what happened," Ben said. "Did I get hit on the head or something? It's like this gray patch in my mind that's just spreading and spreading."

"That's normal," Eleanor assured him. She patted his shoulder. "You probably won't remember any of it. But you saved Naomi. You didn't know what was happening and you still did the right thing."

"That's good, then," he said. He grunted in frustration, gripping his head. "I can't fight it. I'm sorry, Eleanor. I'm trying. I—"

"Don't," she said. Sadness rose and fell in her like the soft rhythm of calm seas. "I know. You'd help if you could. But I'd rather you stay safe, and this is usually safer. Go to breakfast. By the time you get to the house you'll probably have some hilarious story about why you're covered in mud in your boxers."

He laughed weakly and stood. "Is there any way I can—?"

"No. Just go," Eleanor told him, and gave him a little push. In his suggestible state, that's all it took. He headed off across the field.

And then there were two.

"Well," Aunt Josephine said softly. Her voice was subdued,

utterly unlike her. Spackled in mud, she looked not at all like herself, and in a way that was more frightening than if she'd had an obvious wound. "This explains a few things."

"Does it?" Pip asked.

"I thought I was . . ." Aunt Josephine trailed off. "I couldn't run away from this town fast enough. But even out there, I saw things. And then I'd have to move on again."

"You are attuned to the otherworldly, aren't you?" Jack asked. "I wondered. Normally the People Who Look Away have a hard time influencing those ignorant of them, but Mrs. Prosper's control over you was quick and total."

"It's really all real," Aunt Josephine said wonderingly. "I thought there was something wrong with me."

"I thought that, too," Eleanor said. "Until I met Pip and Otto."

"I had almost convinced myself there must be a normal explanation for it all," Mr. Maughan said. It was the first he'd spoken since they emerged. "Austin is dead, isn't he?"

"I'm sorry," Eleanor said. "I wish we could have saved him."

"I never thought that I could rescue him. I only wanted to know what had happened," Mr. Maughan said. Mr. Maughan hesitated. "Is Caspian . . ." He looked too afraid to finish the question.

"Oh! He's fine," Eleanor said quickly. "He's at my house, eating socks."

"Thank goodness," Mr. Maughan said.

Aunt Josephine put an arm around Pip's shoulder. "Let's get

you back home. And then I want to know exactly what happened here," she said. "And who this gentleman is." She eyed Jack with unconcealed curiosity.

"Jack," he said, sweeping a bow. And then, gravely and deliberately, "I am Eleanor's father. If you stay in town, I'm sure you'll be seeing a great deal of me, as I won't be going anywhere."

Eleanor let out a strangled noise, neither a laugh nor a sob. He nodded to her deeply.

"You get to be a real person now," Pip said, her smile crooked and sorrowful.

"It is not worth the price" was his bitter reply. "I am sorry. I searched so hard for a way to lift the story. Bartimaeus warned me it was likely fruitless."

Wait. Bartimaeus. "Bartimaeus Ashford had a message for you," Eleanor said, suddenly remembering. "On Halloween, he said that if I saw my father, I should tell him something."

Jack's brows lifted. "And what was that?"

"He said to tell you that the answer was 'Yes.' So—what was the question?" Eleanor asked.

Jack smiled, and gave a low, warm chuckle. "The question was, 'Can the curse of the Prime Stories be broken?'" he said. "I wanted to know if I could end them, not merely pass them along."

"Then it's possible," Pip said, hope in her voice once again.

"If Bartimaeus was right," Eleanor said.

"He's right," Otto said firmly. "And if he can figure it out, so can we. I mean, he's old, but he's not that smart. Or he would've figured out a way to break the Curse of Thirteens by now, too."

"Oh, we're *way* smarter than Bartimaeus," Pip agreed with a firm nod.

"Hold on. I think I'm going to need a bit of a history lesson here," Aunt Josephine said, holding up a plaintive hand.

"Don't worry. We'll catch you up," Pip promised. She took her aunt's arm. "Let's go home. All of us."

She and Otto and Josephine started off, Mr. Maughan stumbling along beside them. Eleanor looked at Jack. "Come on," she said. "Let's go home."

"Home?" he echoed.

"Where else would you stay?" she asked. "You're family. And we definitely have the room."

She stuck out her hand. And after a moment's hesitation, her dad took it.

"Your mother would be very proud of you," he told her.

"I know," she said. "And she will be. When we get her back."

Together, they followed the others. And Eleanor tried, very hard, not to notice that when Otto glanced back at her and the light flashed over his eyes, they weren't the soft, warm brown they should have been.

They were gray.

Epilogue

"Got it! Now!" Eleanor said, bracing herself against the suit-case that threatened to bulge out of the hatchback.

Pip swung the door down and Eleanor ducked out of the way just in time to avoid getting brained. They both had to heave against it, the surface hot in the early summer sun, to get the latch to click, but then it was done, all the suitcases were in the car, and the car didn't immediately explode, so they high-fived in victory.

"Got it!" Pip called. Aunt Josephine had just stepped out of the house and clapped her hands in appreciation. "Just don't open any doors or take any hard curves and I think everything should stay put until you hit Vancouver."

The car almost groaned, stuffed wall to wall with boxes and bags—somehow even more than Josephine had arrived with, and that was before Mr. Maughan's suitcases and Caspian's car-rier got added in.

Josephine swept Pip up in a hug. "Are you sure I shouldn't stay?"

"We'll be fine," Pip promised. "Besides, you've been here for almost three months already. I think if you stick around any longer, Dad might *actually* lose it."

"I am a bit much," Aunt Josephine conceded with a laugh. "But I promise you, I'm still going to help. Mathew and I are going to learn everything we can about these Wrong Things and then we'll be back."

Mr. Maughan emerged, carrying a flailing but happy Caspian. "Ready to go, my dear?" he asked.

"All set," Josephine told him, beaming. They'd been inseparable since the Wickerwood. He was a far cry from a cowboy, but then, Josephine never liked being predictable.

They said their final farewells, and Eleanor and Pip stood in the driveway waving as Aunt Josephine and Mr. Maughan pulled away and drove down the road, Caspian yapping happily through the back window. Pip let out a soft sigh.

"Are you going to miss her?" Eleanor asked.

"Of course. But three months is a *lot* of Aunt Jojo," Pip said. "And honestly, it's been pretty weird having an adult around who knows about the Wrong Things."

That much was true. Aunt Josephine couldn't get used to the fact that she couldn't just step in and fix things for them, be the "grown-up." Something they would have given anything for a few months ago but now just got in the way.

They knew what they were doing as much as anyone could. And this was their story, not Aunt Josephine's.

Their story. And that was another reason they wanted Aunt Josephine gone. She hadn't noticed yet the way Pip was changing. Some things subtly, some things less so—like the way her irises had turned a flat, slate gray. Or how she'd grown three inches in six weeks, and now had actual *muscles*.

They'd break the curse. And in the meantime, maybe it would be useful. Eleanor didn't hate the idea of having a sword-wielding warrioress for a co–best friend.

At least that was the story she told herself, so that she could sleep at night.

Eleanor stretched, working out the kinks in her shoulders from hauling all of Aunt Josephine's luggage. She turned—and shrieked.

A woman stood directly behind her. Black hair hung to the middle of her back. Her skin was pale, her eyes slate gray, and around her neck hung a sapphire set in silver that winked in the sun. She stood at the end of a road—a road that somehow stretched straight through Pip's house and beyond, even though the house was still there, standing as strong and sturdy as ever.

The only reason Eleanor didn't run was that Otto was standing next to her.

"Hey, Pip. Eleanor," he said, his eyes—his eyes that were more and more often just a little bit gray—wide. "This is the world walker, and she'd like a word."

Eleanor looked down. The woman's hands were clasped in front of her. Hands that were turned the wrong way around on her wrists, palms out where they should be in. She wasn't looking at Eleanor at all. She was staring at Pip.

"Jack," the woman said warmly. Her voice had an odd echo to it, as if it were coming from inside a tunnel. "It's so good to see you again. I have come to tell you: the Wending is open. We have work to do."

Acknowledgments

In a very difficult year, this book has brought me comfort and purpose. So many people have supported its creation and kept me going over the past months.

I would first like to extend a special thanks to Mathew Murakami, half of Mr. Maughan's namesake and one of my favorite people in the world. When I named Mr. Maughan after Mat, I had no idea that months later, as I edited a tale of one Mathew being trapped in an enchanted slumber, Mathew Murakami would be in a coma, their future uncertain. It is with profound joy that I write these words now, knowing that they are still with us and that they will someday be able to read this.

Mat, from the very first time we met, you have been a generous and kind friend. I am endlessly grateful to have you in my life and my kids' lives. You make the world a better place with your enthusiasm, your thoughtfulness, your creativity, and your storytelling. I love you, friend. You've got so many stories left to tell, most importantly your own, and I am so thankful that you get to.

I should also thank Patrick Maughan again, the other half of that namesake and the man who provided the spark of an idea that became *Thirteens*. And to the rest of the Wednesday night crew: Petri Mulhauser, Andy Smith, and Michelle Mallet, for your companionship and creativity.

The No Name Writing Group were as always instrumental in turning a dubious heap of words into something resembling a finished draft. To Shanna Germain, Erin M. Evans, Susan Morris, Rhiannon Held, and Corry L. Lee—you rock. Special thanks to Corry and her husband, Josh, for letting me borrow their brilliant "Kung Poo Fighting" song, a staple of the changing table in our household.

My family is probably way past being impressed when I put them in the acknowledgments, but still—Mom, Dad, Rosemary, Mike, Other Mike: thank you, for all you do. (Especially you, Mouse.)

And finally, to everyone at Viking who's knocked it out of the park on every front once again, starting with my brilliant editor, Maggie Rosenthal; designers Maria Fazio and Kate Renner; cover artist Juliette Brocal; as well as Marinda Valenti, Abigail Powers, and Sola Akinlana. I never get tired of handing all of you a story and getting back a book.